About the Author

Mathew Vincent Menacherry is a co-founder of the Anthea Group, which is active in the field of speciality chemicals. He lives in Mumbai with his wife, Candice, and their daughter, Shanaia.

Feni Daze is his second novel.

FENI DAZE

DEAR DAVID,
HOPE YOU ENJOY THIS.
WARMLY,
MATHEW

M   OCT 5, 2019

Mathew Vincent Menacherry

FENI DAZE

Vanguard Press

A CIP catalogue record for this title is
available from the British Library.

ISBN 978-1-78465-501-3

*Vanguard Press is an imprint of
Pegasus Elliot MacKenzie Publishers Ltd.*
www.pegasuspublishers.com

First Published in 2019

**Vanguard Press
Sheraton House Castle Park
Cambridge England**

Printed & Bound in Great Britain

Dedication

To the memory of my friend and brother,
Jojo the Gent

PROLOGUE

The worst thing about having a drunk for a father is not the abuse. The whippings, the humiliation, the constant state of turmoil, all these I could handle, but what troubled me most was the inevitable nose-dive into penury.

We started off in an apartment, a rather nice one, I think, though my memories of this phase are nebulous. This was when my mother was still around, but after she left, I tried my best to erase all traces of her.

Not so the pater. He moped and wailed, then lost his job as a junior accountant and went back to his first love with a vengeance.

The problem, I realised, was that she was always too good for him. And our modest, middle-class existence didn't gel with her notions of happily ever after.

He, of course, blamed me for her leaving. Apparently, things were just fine till I popped out, and then proceeded steadily downhill. Sure, they'd always had their rows, about how little he earned, and how she was forced to stay in Mahakali while her sister was living it up in Bandra. But these were trivial lovers' tiffs compared to what came later, or so I was repeatedly told.

The sister, my aunt, was a stewardess working for the national carrier, who had, predictably, married a flyboy on his second go around. This was after the fool had been caught by his first wife bonking my aunt on a layover. After much screeching and fisticuffs, a divorce was hammered out, followed almost immediately by a wedding. There are wimps in this world who can't stomach spending a single minute alone.

It was at her place that my mum, during a sabbatical from my dad, met her second hubby, a commander with the same airline. Sparks flew, the inevitable happened, and my dad was out on his arse with me in tow.

She called me once, years later, after she was diagnosed with cancer. Was suitably teary and repentant, which didn't go down very well with me. I was brusque and cold, and I'm sure she hung up the phone wondering why she'd even bothered. She shouldn't have, really. You don't fuck up the life of a ten-year-old and then make a call over twenty years later to say you're sorry. You ought to take that sort of stuff to the grave, which is only fair.

CHAPTER 1

Ennui: A feeling of weariness and discontent resulting from satiety or lack of interest.

It was the right word... *le mot juste*, as Flaubert so succinctly put it... apt in a sense that it summed up what I was going through then.

***

I walked out of the drab edifice that posed as an airport in Dabolim to find Ana, pressed up against a waist-high barrier, waving out to me. She had dropped a few kilos and looked stunning in a short denim dress that seemed familiar. I knew I was meant to recognise it, place it in an appropriate memory slot, but I couldn't.

It was a fabulous morning. The sky was a pale shade of unbroken blue and even the rainclouds had stayed away. The sun was out and it was pleasantly warm, and I was glad to be there.

We linked arms, hers around mine, and walked to a junk heap parked in the shade of a few trees a little distance away. The driver stirred as we approached and then swung out of the cab like an orang-utan. He was a geriatric, and reeked of the drink. Smarmy in a way that old men get in a place like this.

'Vic, this is Uncle Joe,' Ana said. 'I've been using him since yesterday.'

Uncle Joe, who'd been used since yesterday, grinned toothlessly and held out a sweaty paw, which I took in mine (very briefly).

'He's quite a character,' she whispered, as she snuggled up to me in the back seat. 'Maybe you could write about him.'

'Maybe,' I drawled, doing my Bogie bit, 'but right now I'd rather do something else.'

'Like what?' she simpered, and then kissed me. And it almost seemed like the old days.

***

The drive to Baga from Dabolim seemed interminable to me. There was a feeling of rawness at the back of my throat that I knew intimately.

'Ana, ask him to stop at a liquor store.'

'*Now*?' she yelped, as if buying booze was the last thing folks did on holiday.

'Yeah,' I replied.

'Vic, can't it wait till we reach the resort? You have the next three days here, you know.' A nascent whine had crept into her tone, which annoyed me.

'Joe,' I reached forward and tapped his bony shoulder, 'need a drink, men. Is there a wine shop on the way?'

Joe grinned like a deranged ape, displaying all five of his teeth in the mirror. Clearly, we were on his turf.

'Not on this route, men, not for a bit, but take a swig of this. Good shtuff.'

It *was* good shtuff, I concurred, as I took a sip from the Pepsi bottle which contained the *feni*, ready-mixed with soda and ready to go. Just what a cabbie needed on those lonesome stretches, and rules and stats both be damned.

Ana was silent, her face pressed up against the window, away from me. I think her eyes were brimming, though I couldn't be sure. I took a few more sips and slid closer.

'Hey,' I said.

'Hey,' she replied, turning her head and fixing me with those hazel orbs, and I felt a wee bit like the way I'd felt before. Then she kissed me on the neck and laid her head on my chest, and I stroked her hair and thought of another girl.

***

I sipped from the bottle for most of the journey, while she dozed with her head on my thigh. She slept like she always did, easily and without effort. She had told me once that she never dreamed. It was a trick I'd always wanted to learn from her.

I caught Joe's eyes in the mirror and held them for a while. I'd been in Goa on several occasions and knew the type, though Ana, with her typical guilelessness, appeared quite taken in. She had drifted below his line of sight and I knew the perv was struggling to figure out what she was doing there. He had tried sitting upright in his seat, adjusting the mirror to all angles and turning half around to ask me questions, but still no cigar. He finally quit when he heard her snoring.

'Baby is tired,' he volunteered, and for a moment I wondered whose baby he was talking about. 'She came very late last night.'

I gave him a half-smile and looked away, not wishing to start a conversation.

The roads were pitted and fractured post the monsoon onslaught and it took us almost two hours to get to Baga. Ana had woken up, the Pepsi bottle had been drained and returned to its owner, and I was feeling a whole lot better.

It was the perfect time to be in Goa: the end of September, before the glut of tourists, both *desi* and foreign, made the place quite unbearable. This was of course in the old days, when Goa still had off-seasons. Now I hear that it's always rocking, on one pretext or another.

The taxi pulled into one of those middling properties that line the beaches in Goa. I had assumed that we'd be staying at Cavala, where we'd put up in the past, but Ana had done the bookings this time around.

'There's a pool at the back; hope you've brought your trunks,' Ana said. She was worried about what I'd think of the place and was trying her best to be chipper.

'Our room has an AC, but no TV,' she added.

Now *that* could turn out to be a problem, I thought. No TV meant more conversation, which simply increased the chance of rows, something I for one could do without.

On the way to our cottage we walked past the veranda of the main building, where an old lady sat sprawled out on a recliner. She was browsing through a fashion magazine and sipping from a glass. It was what I loved most about Goa. The time of day meant nothing when it came to tanking up. Ana smiled at her as we passed, but not in her usual heartfelt way. There was history there, I thought.

'Your boyfriend?' asked the crone, looking me up and down. Ana nodded slightly, a tad embarrassed.

'Good-looking bugger,' she muttered, and went back to her article.

'That's Aunty Miranda,' Ana informed me. 'She owns the resort.'

'She's a real character,' she added.

I nodded, wondering how total strangers had assumed pride of place in Ana's family... first Uncle Joe and now Aunty Miranda.

Maybe she's lonely, I thought, and then wished it wasn't so.

Miranda and Joe were characters for sure, but the place was teeming with folks like them (and me, to be honest)... chumps who dive into a bottle at the crack of dawn and then spend the entire day trying to be other people.

There was a time when I was attracted to the type, but it tends to get old, and eventually insufferable. There's nothing edifying about drool, or drunken blather, and it only seems that way to those who haven't experienced it much.

***

Our room turned out to be slightly better than I'd expected. Ana hails from a wealthy family in Bangalore, but her idea of a holiday was slumming it in the pokiest joints she could find. This was great while we were dating, when I would insist on shelling out my half. Those days, however, were long gone now. She had even sent me the flight tickets.

The furniture was mostly cane and quite comfortable. There were tell-tale stains on the sheets, though, as is common in love nests like this. The room had a musty odour, which lessened somewhat when we opened the windows.

'You slept *here* last night?' I asked. It was some distance away from the main building, and Ana is not the bravest person I know.

'Aunty put me up in another room… closer to the lobby. This one's costlier.'

There it was again, the unstated message… I am okay with doing without… I can manage with whatever little you earn.

I was younger then and it galled me, though it had no reason to.

I dropped my haversack on the ground and took her in my arms before she could say anything more. We threw off our clothes and made love for what seemed like hours, before drifting off to sleep.

CHAPTER 2

I awoke first, with a heavy head and a parched sensation at the back of my throat. Joe's *feni* had begun acting up and I could feel the onset of a headache. I crawled out of bed and reached for a pitcher placed on a side table. The water had a plasticky sweetness to it, but I downed some anyway.

Then, book in hand, I hunkered down on one of the cane armchairs in the room. I was re-reading *Factotum* by Bukowski, about a booze hound named Hank Chinaski, who (at the time) was one of my heroes.

After a while I tossed aside the novel and began flipping through the New Testament, which always seems to show up in dumps like this. This was even more depressing and pretty soon I was back on the bed, spooned up against Ana, trying hard (no pun intended) to wake her.

'Hey, sweetheart, get up,' I whispered in her ear. 'It's evening… we need to head out.'

Ana arose grumpily, shuffled to the bathroom, slammed the door shut and didn't come out for half an hour. When she finally emerged, she looked ravishing in a towel that just about covered the strategic areas.

We made love again, gently this time, and when we were done, I lay back on the crumpled sheets and wished that I could love her more.

'Aren't you going to shower?' she asked, as I slipped into my jeans.

'When we get back,' I replied. 'Have to leave, or all the joints will be shut.'

'In *Goa*?' she said, and I grinned at her. Things were good between us, at least for now.

***

Aunty Miranda was still at it when we passed the lobby on our way out, only now she was seated next to another relic who appeared to be her spouse.

This gent, not surprisingly, had had enough of his wife's company and he pleaded with us to stay for a drink. I would've begged off, but Ana had already stepped up onto the veranda. She gave the geezer a peck on the cheek and introduced him to me as Uncle Jack, co-owner of the resort, and the one it had been named after — Captain Jack's.

'You're a writer or what?' he asked. Word had clearly got around.

'What,' I muttered.

Ana placed her hand on my forearm and I shrugged it off. This had always been a sore point between us. She claimed that I was withdrawn and often rude to strangers, and her need to bond with even the measliest wretch on the planet irked me immensely. I didn't realise, not then anyway, that I too would never have made the cut had it been any different.

We sat around with Jack and Miranda for as long as I could take it and then, perhaps abruptly, I got up to leave. I'd already downed two glasses of their *feni*, and it was vile stuff. I shuddered to think what it would do to me later.

'What's your hurry, men?' Jack asked, crestfallen, and I couldn't really blame him. I would have put a slug through my own head if I had to spend the rest of my days with Miranda.

The lady in question was glaring at me. She'd been giving Ana the lowdown on her daughter-in-law in Miami, who was Puerto Rican and who detested her, never even allowing their own son to come visit. Ana had been nodding in earnest and making all the right noises while the crone prattled on, but I could see that she, too, was bored.

'We have to meet up with some friends, actually,' she said, unconvincingly.

***

'How can you call yourself a writer when you're so closed to new experiences?' she chided, as we headed to the shacks on the beach. I slipped my arm around her.

'I just wanted to be alone with *you*,' I said, and she giggled and moved in closer.

We had reached the main street that led to the beach, and the lights and the shacks and the cheap booze I knew was in there perked up my mood considerably.

'Want to step in for a quick one?' I asked, pointing to the very first dive at the corner.

'Vic, can we keep walking? There's a better one just down the road. It's called Parry's. My friends were raving about it.'

Her friends were part of the swish set in Bangalore. They frequented joints that were overpriced and loud, and partied with folks like them who they bitched about later. Guys like me were an oddity as far as they were concerned. They treated me like a rare species of primate and appeared fascinated by the fact that I had grown up in a *chawl*. Those were the good days, when I was charming and funny and relatively sober. All that, of course, changed shortly thereafter.

We kept on walking in the direction of the beach. He who pays the piper, I thought nastily.

There was a certain feel to our relationship now, a tautness that hadn't been there earlier. Not that this was surprising, given all that had transpired.

Parry's seemed like just another shack to me, though bigger than many others. It was located right on the beach, which I knew would be quite a draw for the amateur tippler. There were large screens suspended from the thatch roof, which I found out was for karaoke on weekends. It was early by Baga's partying standards and the place was relatively tranquil. I figured we could stay for a while before heading out.

I walked over to a stool and asked the seemingly under-age barkeep to fix me a *feni* and soda (when in Rome and all that). Ana clambered awkwardly onto a bar stool beside mine and ordered a pina colada. She would've preferred a corner table, away from the music, but I couldn't go through the charade of having a meaningful conversation with her.

I knew why she'd wanted to meet up in Goa. It was the clichéd last shot, and it hadn't started off too badly either. At least we weren't screaming at each other.

***

The barkeep was called Domingo and he was all of sixteen, as I had guessed. Anywhere else he would've

22

been out of a job and the establishment fined and shuttered, but not in Goa. He had quit school after flunking the eighth standard thrice in a row, and had no plans of going back.

'They teach all crap there, men. Whaddafuck will I *do* with geometry and algebra?' he asked.

I concurred. Besides, he was getting a richer education right there in the bar.

Ana had also warmed to him and began probing delicately about his family. Did they know that he worked here? Didn't they mind?

They knew, he informed us, and they didn't mind at all. The manager was a relative and Domingo's wages were delivered to their house on the fifth of every month, completely deducted at source as far as he was concerned.

Domingo didn't mind either. He survived on tips, as did all the others. *Goras* tipped handsomely, but *desis* not as much, he said, looking at me meaningfully. I looked across meaningfully as well, at Ana, who seemed determined to correct this imbalance.

The hustle had started, as was inevitable, but it was subtle and quite well done for a sixteen-year-old.

After a while he quit jabbering about his family when he sensed that I was tuning out. He didn't know that I would not be the one settling our tab. After a short lull in the conversation, he began mouthing off again, this time about his job and the long hours he worked during the season.

'I sleep for only three hours a day, men, for almost four months.'

How, I asked.

'See, this place winds up by around four in the morning, and then if I get lucky with some *gori* pussy, I go to her room to fuck her... or we do it on the beach sometimes.'

'You get lucky often?' I queried, intrigued now. I could feel Ana tapping my shin with her foot. She thought I was mocking him, but I wasn't. I really needed to know.

'During peak season... almost every night, men. They *throw* themselves at us.' He grinned.

I studied his visage carefully, the rotting teeth and the unibrow, and not for the first time I marvelled at the wondrous properties of alcohol.

'You have to know how to talk to them,' he went on, 'and then we also mix their drinks. At two in the morning, the fuck they care if they're drinking Bacardi or Smirnoff.'

It was the age-old Goan serenade. I wondered whether he was mixing *our* drinks. Ana, I knew, wouldn't be able to tell the difference, but she wasn't much of a drinker anyway. And I was on *kaju feni*, and you couldn't switch *that* with anything else.

'We only do it to *goris* who like us,' he concluded, sensing that he'd shot his mouth off.

I wanted to pursue this line of thinking, but I could see that Ana was upset. She began looking around for other folks to talk to. Domingo, too, was keeping his gob shut for the time being.

All of a sudden, we heard a commotion and turned to see what it was. An electric blue Pajero had pulled up outside the bar, windows rolled down and reggae music blaring.

The engine was turned off and five youths stepped out of the vehicle. They were clad in what conventionally would be termed as party gear. Four of them sported bandannas and the fifth, presumably the leader, was wearing a white Stetson. He had been at the wheel of the SUV and walked into the shack as if he owned it.

This guy took a quick look around and then figured that the little action there was (in the form of Ana) was at the counter, and so they all trooped up and perched on bar stools right next to us.

The leader was tall and appeared to have just begun training with weights. His physique was in that in-between stage of the novice bodybuilder, mostly soft, but with a hint of muscle in all the obvious places. He had also brought along his gym instructor, it appeared. This lad was short but built like a rhino, with a disproportionately large chest and shoulders.

He was wearing a black netted T-shirt that showed off an admirable six-pack. The catch of the day, I whispered to Ana, who giggled.

'Who's the arsehole?' I asked Domingo, as he refilled my drink.

'Nobody, men, just a rich man's son,' that poet whispered.

Turned out he was a very rich man's son. His daddy owned iron ore mines in Goa and his uncle was the Tourism Minister, which was probably why they were fawning all over him in the bar.

Not so my man Domingo, who had a set expression on his face as he served them their drinks. Maybe Richie Rich was a poor tipper, I thought, unlike the *goras*.

The mating ritual commenced and it was as galling as ever. Ana was easily the prettiest girl in the joint and Mr Stetson began eyeing her. He wasn't too subtle about it either. He had a fixed half-smile on his face as his eyes bored into her like laser pointers. I wouldn't have minded, but he was making her very uncomfortable, and this was pissing me off. I caught his eye and nodded my head from side to side, and the smile withered on his mug. It could've been the scar on my cheek, or the busted snout, but it killed his mood for sure. No one can afford to be glassed in the gut, rich daddy or not.

He wouldn't let it rest, though, and whispered something to his pit bull, who then felt compelled to do the staring. I glanced at this lad and all his muscles bunched up. Very nice, I thought, very scary.

I had already picked out the bottle I'd use and was just about to say something when Ana stood up. She held my face with both hands and whispered, 'Vic, let's just leave, *please*.'

I would've done things differently, but it was her holiday, and so I slipped off the bar stool as she settled the tab and received one of those intricate grabbing, patting, finger-snapping handshakes from Domingo, which was quite the rage in those days. Ana tipped him extravagantly, *gori*-style, and I let the hustle pass.

'You make the *best* pina coladas,' she said to Domingo, with her palm on his cheek, and I swear the dark little bastard blushed.

The group got a bit more vocal as we moved towards the exit. There were catcalls and hooting and one of them did a pretty good chicken impersonation, flapping arms and all.

I was hoping that they'd follow us out, but this didn't happen.

CHAPTER 3

A few months after my mother left, Ammama moved in with us.

Ammama was a short, reticent lady, armed with a faint moustache and an over-used rosary, and to look at her no one could tell that there was a phase in her life when she had gone off the rails.

Her father was a ticketing clerk in Ernakulam North railway station and it was here that she came into contact with Samson Gabriel, a swashbuckling Anglo-Indian who had been transferred to Ernakulam as a supervisor. Ammama could never be considered a beauty by any definition, but she did possess a homely charm that some men find attractive. To add to this, in Samson's case, there was no pressing need for discernment, as for him it was merely a pleasant diversion until he rejoined his wife and daughters in Ratlam.

My dad was the unfortunate result of this dalliance, and when the mighty Samson realised what he had done, he promptly abandoned his post and headed north.

I guess you could say that she was the one who took care of me, at least for a while. She was also forced to take care of her full-grown son, who by then had been reduced to a sodden, blubbering mess.

His company finally terminated him when he began hitting the bottle at work. Our savings ran out shortly thereafter, and we were forced to sell our flat in Model Town and move into a two-room tenement in the nearby MHADA colony. After the apartment was disposed of and the housing loan settled, there was a small sum left over, and this was what we survived on each time my dad was thrown out of yet another job.

When my mum was around, he had insisted that I attend Holy Family, which was one of the better schools in the area. I used to be a pretty decent student, but after she vamoosed something just died inside me. It didn't destroy me, as it did my fool of a father, but it still snuffed out something within. I lost all interest in studies, started hanging out with older, poorer and more violent kids, and began making a mess of my life.

My dad was summoned to the school on numerous instances and always failed to show up, save on the first occasion, when I was caught smoking in the loo.

'Mr Gabriel, your son Victor was apprehended smoking cigarettes in the boys' toilet,' our dickhead of a vice-principal, Father Innocent, informed the shipwreck seated in front of him. This worthy, my *paterfamilias*, an AA veteran who by then had relapsed to his former state, glared at me in a mixture of shame and disbelief. It was quite a performance from the very same gent whose pants I had to pull off just a couple of nights earlier because he'd peed in them in his sleep.

'Is this *true*?' he asked theatrically, and I wondered whether he'd downed a few before showing up here.

I remained silent.

'I asked you a question, Vic-terrr,' the chump went on. 'Is this *troooo*?'

I failed to see what all the fuss was about. So, I'd inhaled some tobacco smoke. It was a lot better than swallowing crap all your life and then puking it up on your family, just because they were the only ones who would take it from you.

Still I said nothing. The fool's eyes were rolling around in his head, and I *knew* he'd been hitting the bottle.

Father Innocent was, to put it mildly, loving it. Christian Charity and Forgiveness could both be damned as far as he was concerned. Here was a Soul That Needed Saving, and *that* was far more important than the lesser tenets of his religion.

I should've seen the blow coming, but I didn't, partly because I never imagined that the chump would strike me in front of a priest. It was a hard one (he still had some of his strength in those days) and it threw me off the chair and left me sprawled out on the floor.

He glanced at the priest, perhaps expecting to be reprimanded, but all he saw on that porcine mug was encouragement, rabid delight at witnessing the Devil being given his due. In Father Innocent's eyes this was definitely a dad who knew how to raise his son.

Goaded on, the chump rose from his seat and began unbuckling his belt. I curled up into a foetal pose, as I'd learnt to do at a young age, and had already exited the room when the blows began to fall.

Father Innocent waited until enough strokes had been landed to banish Lucifer from the premises. Then, as if in shocked outrage, he sprang up from his seat, grabbed the moron by his arm and screamed, 'Stop, Mr Gabriel. Stop this at *once*. The boy has learnt his lesson.'

I peeked up at the dope and saw him glaring at me, perhaps wondering if I had indeed learnt my lesson.

'Take him home now, and make sure that this kind of behaviour is not repeated,' the priest intoned.

'I will, Father. Take it from me, this boy will never stray again.'

***

The chump was oddly subdued on the bus ride home, deeply ashamed, I could see. This, of course, was not enough. I had in fact learnt a valuable lesson, just not the one they'd tried to teach me.

And now it was time for him to do some learning.

I waited until Ammama had settled down for the night. I was in charge of laying out her medicines, and I'd added an extra sleeping pill, a very mild dose, so she'd be spared what was coming.

He was watching the news on Doordarshan when I crept up behind him with a cricket stump. I'd aimed for the back of his head, but he turned just as I swung and I caught him square on the temple. He toppled over and bounced off the centre table, and I prayed that Ammama was still out.

He was conscious throughout the beating and moaned and mewed as I pounded him, too drunk to protect himself, and too scared to resist.

'I'm sorry, *mone*,' he mouthed repeatedly.

'You touch me once more, just *once* more, and I'll kill you,' I said, and meant it.

He never raised his hands to me again.

A few years after this, I was expelled from Holy Family. Father Innocent had tried summoning my dad on several occasions, but the chump never bothered to show up. Finally, when even a telegram went unanswered, I was called to the principal's office, given a letter addressed to Wilfred Gabriel, and told to stop attending school forthwith. I guess there was only so much that even men of God could endure.

Luckily for me, Ammama had a cousin who was a high-ranking Salesian priest, and this gent, who I'd never even met, pulled some strings to get me enrolled in the nearby St Dominic Savio School in Sher-e-Punjab.

My new school was focused on sports to the exclusion of almost everything else, and I took to football and hockey with enough enthusiasm to keep me out of trouble. Also, now that the beatings at home had subsided, I found it less of a need to play up at school (spare the rod and all that crap notwithstanding).

I captained our football team and we won the inter-school tournament two years in a row. The priests all loved me and even my mediocre showing in studies was glossed over.

At home, though, things were still lousy, but more of that later.

CHAPTER 4

Arms linked, we walked along the beach in the direction of the river. The sea wind and the alcohol did their thing and soon we were necking furiously. We collapsed on the sand and would have had a go right there if we hadn't heard voices approaching.

I held her in my arms and for a while it seemed as if nothing had changed. She had her head on my shoulder, and I loathed myself for not loving her more.

'Why can't things be different?' she asked.

I said nothing. There wasn't much to say anyway.

'Why, Vic?' she persisted.

'I, being poor, have only my dreams,' I replied, quoting Yeats, always more comfortable in someone else's words.

'You *know* I don't care about that,' she said, and it was true, for the time being. But she was young, and things would change. This I knew.

'I will never, ever love anyone as much as I love you. You realise that, don't you?' she said, and I nodded mutely.

These are words I treasure even now, after all these years.

***

The season had not yet set in and there were very few shacks and restaurants lining the periphery of the beach. I needed a drink badly, and we headed towards a beacon of light in the darkness.

It was a joint called Hemingway's, and made for a pleasant change from the Mambo's, Toto's and Lobo's that littered the beaches in Goa. The place was done up in a seafaring motif and outside were large canoes illuminated with kerosene lamps, with planks of wood laid crossways which served as tables.

A few couples, *goras* mostly, gazed at one another while perching awkwardly on stools placed in these canoes. Luckily for me, I had my arm around Ana's waist and dragged her inside before any fancy notions got to her. The *feni* had begun playing up and I needed a chair with a backrest.

The interiors were also done up in a maritime theme. There were oars, anchors, spyglasses and sextants displayed all over. My favourite touch was a blown-up snap of the Old Man, standing at the stern of a boat, bare-chested and defiant. One of his quotes was pasted below — about how all good books were alike in that they are truer than if they had really happened.

It was crowded inside and we had to hang around for a table. Just as I was considering heading to the bar for a *nippen*, we were shepherded over to a tiny table by the harried maître d'.

'This is a very nice footstool, but where's our *table*?' I asked, and Ana giggled.

'It's one of the best tables in the house, sir,' he informed me curtly; 'you can watch the karaoke from here.'

And it was true — a large screen was suspended from the ceiling quite close to where we were seated, and you could take in all the talent, assuming, of course, that that was what you wanted to do.

All I wanted was another drink.

'When does it *start*?' squealed Ana over the surrounding din, as if listening to drunken Elvises and over-the-hill Celine Dions was by far the most exciting thing to do in Goa.

I summoned a waiter over.

'What're you having?' I asked Ana.

'Vic, you could sing for me,' she teased, but hopefully. A few years back, in a joint like this, I had come up with a passable rendition of *Nikita*. A lifetime ago, it seemed now.

Thankfully, our drinks arrived and I slugged down mine and ordered another.

'So, what are you working on?' she asked. Back when we were dating, this was the first thing she would have said to me, the very first thing on her mind. Now it was almost as if she, too, had stopped believing. I felt vaguely insulted, though I had no reason to feel that way.

'Nothing special,' I replied. 'A couple of short stories.'

There was nothing more to be said, and so both of us said nothing and instead focused on our drinks.

After a while, determined to break the mood, she looked at me and smiled.

'So, do you miss it?'

'What?' I asked. I was still wallowing in my hurt, wading around, testing its edges.

'The Army, silly.'

'No, not really,' I replied.

It had been years ago, before I'd even met up with Ana. And the truth was, the only thing I missed was the cheap booze, and perhaps a few of my buddies in the Rifles — the crazier ones, who could win you battles but would never make CO.

She was trying hard to be cheerful, to engage me in conversation, when all I wanted was to be left alone.

'So, what do you think about these two?' she asked in her broken Malayalam, and grudgingly I turned to look.

It was a game we used to play. It'd started out by her remarking that as a writer I needed to be adept at sizing up folks in a single glance. I used to be pretty good at it in those days.

She was pointing discreetly at a couple of ladies seated at the table next to ours. The place was so packed that our tables were almost touching. If a waiter tried to scurry through, he would've had to do it sideways, with his butt on our table and his balls on theirs, or vice versa.

I studied the women for a while. They appeared to be in their early forties or thereabouts.

The younger one caught me staring and turned to give me a look, a very direct one, I thought. I smiled at her and she turned away, not displeased.

'Sisters,' I said authoritatively, which they clearly were, although the elder one had crossed the stage at which some women begin to resemble men.

'And?' Ana asked.

'Loaded,' I pronounced. 'Wives of NRI industrialists, here on their own for some R&R.'

Turned out they were hairdressers from Manchester. The elder sis was going through a painful divorce and the younger was there to support her.

***

The karaoke started up soon after and we were forced to listen to a line of screeching bozos scrabbling for their three minutes of fame. The younger sis sent in her chit as well and was handed the mic by a skinny MC who looked like Mick Jagger.

'I'd like to dedicate this song to my darling sister,' she began, pointing at her caricature.

She then proceeded to do an incredible rendition of *I Will Survive*, which brought tears to the eyes of every female in the room, Ana included.

When the song ended, Ana reached across and hugged her, a conversation opener if ever there was one. Soon our tables were joined, introductions made and fresh drinks ordered.

'So, what is it that you do, then?' asked the younger one, her gaze as direct as it had been before.

'He's a writer,' piped in Ana, before I could come up with something more interesting, like male stripper.

'Wow,' said the elder one. 'So what do you write?'

Words, I wanted to say, and sentences, mostly rambling, disjointed ones. Instead, I gave her the stock reply.

'I'm working on a collection of short stories.'

'Have you been published?' she asked, the one question that every aspiring scribbler dreads. I shook my head.

'Not yet, but he will be... he's very talented.' Ana sprang to my defence as always, though she needn't have. I'd stopped caring about what folks thought of my writing anyway (well, almost).

'He was also in the army,' she went on.

'Wow,' said the younger one, clearly more impressed at this line of work. 'So, have you killed anyone?'

'*Jazz*!' yelled her sister, and Ana glanced at me worriedly.

Luckily, there was no further probing into either of my professions, with the next joker on the mic drowning out conversation for a while.

Their names were Margaret and Jaswinder, or Jazz as she referred to herself. Sikh father, English mum, born and brought up in Blighty.

'Call me Marge,' the elder one said, when there was some respite from the singing. 'I can't stand being called Maggie.' I could see why. The resemblance was pretty striking.

I was drinking heavily and the evening had begun to whirl. The sisters were matching me drink for drink and even Ana was consuming more than she usually did. She appeared delighted by the apparent change in my mood.

***

As is common in Goa, intros were made, palms slapped, tables pulled closer, and pretty soon our group was much bigger.

Ana was easily the best-looking girl in the place and all the men were eying her. It was apparent, though, to the most confident buck that she'd be leaving only with me. Consequently, Jazz was the star of the show, and appeared to be enjoying it greatly.

An immense Nigerian was seated next to her, and from where I was perched, I could see that he was pawing her under the table. She didn't seem to mind this, but she was also batting her eyelids at a slim, handsome American who sat facing her. This chappie kept coming up with funny lines, most of them directed at his bigger rival.

The black guy, who called himself Johnny Young (which wasn't, of course, his real name), asked for and was given the mic. This was not a man who was used to waiting in line. I was hoping for some Belafonte, but he picked Ed Grant's *Gimme Hope Jo'anna*. Lots of pent-up angst there, I could see.

They were egging him on, especially the white dude, and our Johnny did not disappoint. His version of *Jo'anna* would've made the absent Eddy cringe. It was a raucous shrieking that went on and on and on.

He was gazing at Jazz as he belted out the number and everyone was cracking up, except me.

I knew what was coming.

'Give him hope, Joanna,' the seated comic said to Jazz, and she went all gooey-eyed. Johnny saw it, too, and his croaking faltered.

There was much cheering when he wound up, a bit abruptly I thought, as there were a few more stanzas remaining. Not that anyone was complaining.

'Give us more, Johnny. One more,' screamed the white guy when the cheers had subsided. I tried making eyes at him, but the fool was on a roll. He had failed to notice Mr Young, who had returned to our table and was looming over him.

'Get up,' said Johnny quietly.

'Hey, *relax*, buddy, we were just kidding,' stammered the American, who was getting a serious case of the runs.

'*Get up!*' bellowed Johnny, and the guy sprang to his feet.

'You insulted me, maan,' Johnny intoned.

'I was joking, buddy, just for laughs... didn't mean to offend you.'

'I treat you with respect, motherfucker. You come to my home and I welcome you with open arms, and then you insult me in front of my friends.' *Home*, I mouthed silently to Ana, and all this while we'd assumed that Johnny was from Lagos.

But Ana wasn't smiling. Her eyes had widened in fear, which was when I decided that enough was enough. I had no problem with Johnny escorting the chump outside and putting a boot in his arse, but scaring my lady and spoiling everyone's evening was an absolute no-no as far as I was concerned.

The white guy's skin tone had changed a few colours by the time I got to my feet. I walked around the table and they were all watching me, Johnny included.

I moved in close and saw him tense up. We were about the same height, but he outweighed me by forty kilos. His shoulders and chest were enormous and barely contained in the tank top he was wearing. The veins in his neck had bulged and stood out like ropes.

But I looked deep into his eyes, and I knew there would be no fighting; not that I cared either way.

I gave him the stare, the blank one, and he saw the evil lurking there. Then, when I knew he'd backed down completely, I gave him back his face.

'Don't do it, bro, you'll kill the fucker.'

'He *insulted* me, maan.'

'I know… I saw it. But let him go this one time, for me. You're ruining a fine evening.'

'He insulted me, maan,' he repeated, but I could see that his heart was not in it.

'Get the fuck out of here, *now*,' I snarled at the white boy, and wisely he bolted.

Honour restored somewhat, Johnny insisted that I join him on the floor, where together we made mincemeat of *Buffalo Soldier*. This time around, the applause went on forever.

***

Post the fracas, our group became a lot smaller, and towards the end it was just Ana, Johnny, me and the sisters.

Hemingway's was closing up for the night and Johnny suggested that we head to Parry's. It was, he pronounced, the most happening joint in Baga, where all the really cool fuckers hung out.

Ana tried protesting, but everyone else was clearly game for more. I assured her that things would be okay, that there wouldn't be any trouble. I was at a point where all I wanted was my next hit of alcohol.

And so, we grope-walked along the beach to Parry's. Johnny was walking in front with his arms around the sisters. He had one meaty paw on Marge's shoulder and the other around Jazz's waist, perilously close to her bum. To me this seemed very unfair. Jazz was happily married, while Marge was the one going through a divorce, as she'd informed us all through the evening. One thing, though, you couldn't fault the big guy for his taste.

I could see that Ana was still apprehensive, and so I did my bit to lighten the mood.

'I wonder which dimwit named this place Parry's?' I said. 'In Goa you would expect a Lisbon, but *Parry's*?'

'Maybe he found love in Paris. Maybe when *you* open a joint like this, you'll call it Bangalore,' she teased.

'Maybe he just got laid in Paris.'

'In which case, you could still call it Bangalore,' she smiled. I drew her in and kissed her, *feni*-breath and all.

'Hey, you guys... get a room or something,' cut in Mr Young, sending Jazz into a paroxysm of giggles. She had reached a point where she found everything he said, hilarious, and I knew they'd be sleeping together.

CHAPTER 5

I managed to scrape through the Tenth Boards and, through a sports quota, got myself admitted to Mithibai College. In the meantime, things at home were proceeding steadily downhill, with Ammama throwing in the towel and scooting off to Kerala.

'I just can't take it any more, *mone*,' she had sobbed on my shoulder on her way out. 'I can't continue living like this, not at my age,' she'd said, looking pointedly at her son, who slouched in a corner in a sullen silence.

'It's okay, Ammama, we'll manage,' I replied, wishing that I, too, had somewhere I could escape to.

Our lives, which were being drained into the sewer of my father's addiction, had descended yet another rung when we were booted out of our MHADA tenement. The chump had run up a huge tab with the mob that operated the liquor *adda* in Majaswadi, and one night a group of them came a-calling.

There were six of them: large, unshaven brutes, some of them brandishing choppers. My dad pissed himself and Ammama nearly had a stroke. One thing led to another, and we were forced to sell our home.

The debt was cleared, with interest, and we moved into a measly space in the nearby Munshi Colony, with common bogs, to boot.

It was these toilets that finally broke Ammama.

It was hard enough for me to stomach, and for her it was an absolute nightmare. Every day she would set her alarm for 5am to try and beat the lines forming outside the loos, only to find that on most mornings she'd still have to wait her turn behind some of the more assiduous residents of the *chawl*.

A few months of this and she threw in the towel.

I never once blamed her for running out on us, and by then I'd even stopped blaming my father. Some things are simply your karma, and you bore them as best as you could. Or you looked to get out, which was what I planned on doing.

***

After we shifted house to Munshi Colony, I did my best to stay away from my father. Watching him kill himself in slow motion was not something I enjoyed, and initially I took to spending more time in college. But after six months of this, I'd learned just one thing — that I didn't want to be there either. I found college more of a drag than being parked at home, and *that* was saying something; but at least at home I had my books, and the tube, on the rare instances that I could pry away the TV remote from him.

My dad by now would start tanking up from the time he surfaced, and I often wondered how he survived for as long as he did. He would perch on his armchair (one of the few things that remained from his marriage) and stare at the screen all day long. Glass in hand, he would eloquently opine on the state of the world, even as the real world passed him by. I would take as much of this as I could and then, book in hand, I'd head for the nearby hills.

In those days, Mahakali Caves was a rustic haven, quite unlike what it has turned into now. The area was littered with hillocks, ponds and streams, and it was a great place to while away time, especially if you were not in need of company.

This was the phase when I began my own tryst with alcohol.

It had started out with stolen sips from his liquor stock, but after a while, when I'd lost all fear of him, we even took to sharing a bottle. Fool that he was, he actually thought of it as some form of father-son bonding.

Enforced poverty had brought about radically differing changes in my dad and me. He had lapsed into a Buddha-like state of mind from which he surfaced only occasionally, while I, on the other hand, had little control over the barrage of emotions that assailed me.

***

There was an illicit brewery operating in the *chawl*, which was quite a draw for all the macho males who resided in the vicinity. It was like having a multiplex next door. Every evening I would hang around there, sharing drinks with these worthies, before returning home with a bottle for my father.

A gang of youths would show up frequently, and over time I began chatting with them. It was led by a lout called Ganesh Mhatre, who was only a couple of years older than me, and rumoured to be close to the local corporator.

I was seventeen at the time and had filled out considerably. I'd also developed a reputation for toughness, though where this came from, I did not know, as I'd always thought of myself as shy and reticent.

One evening, Ganesh walked up to me just as I was taking a last sip from my glass before heading home.

'It's good stuff, no?' he said.

He did have a reputation, and in our world, it paid to be cautious.

'Yeah,' I replied, 'it is.'

'You're that drunkard's son, right?' he asked.

'My father drinks, yeah,' I replied guardedly.

'Doesn't everybody's?' he said, and guffawed.

One thing led to another and pretty soon we began hanging out. The guy had a lot of stuff going on, and he wanted me to get involved. I guess in his line of work it paid to have an English-speaking hoodlum around.

Mostly it entailed a form of gentle extortion, or collection of *hafta*, as it is referred to in the city. Every Friday, a gang of youths would do the rounds of the shops in the vicinity and demand a weekly contribution. Most folks coughed up willingly, as those who didn't were subjected to jibes, vandalism and at times a bit of harassment when their wives and daughters went about their business.

There were other rackets as well — organising Ganpati *mandals*, petty thievery from shops and warehouses in the area, and providing hired muscle when called for, the last of which was the sort of work I fancied. I was seldom a party to stealing, and even the weekly *hafta* duties bored me, but a bit of *hathapayi* was something I looked forward to, and these were usually the jobs that were assigned to me.

***

It all came to an end, though, after an incident in Takshila, a more upmarket housing colony in the neighbourhood.

One of the chumps residing there had got his arse kicked in a bout of fisticuffs with another fella. The matter should've ended there, but, as is often the case, it escalated.

The boy who had received the licking knew Ganesh, as his father, a grocery store owner, had been paying him off for years, and a few days after the incident dad and son (both dimwits, if you ask me) came a-crawling.

It was a scene straight out of *The Godfather*. Ganesh must've only watched Bollywood rip-offs of Coppola's classic, but he played his role to perfection.

'What do you want from me, Ramesh*bhai*?' he intoned, even sounding a bit like old man Vito.

'I want him to bleed, *bhai*, just like he made my son bleed.'

Ganesh paused before replying.

'It will be done, Ramesh*bhai*. Victor here will tell you how much it will cost, but rest assured your work *will* be done.'

I saw the consternation on the grocer's face. He'd assumed, erroneously, that his years of coughing up protection money would entitle him to some when called for. He was already regretting his decision, but there was little he could do about it. Backing off at this point would make him look like a bigger fool, and would also risk arousing Ganesh's ire. And so, grudgingly, he sat down with me to negotiate.

It took almost an hour, during which time Ganesh had to make a few appearances to coax the talks along, but finally we arrived at a figure.

The sum had to be paid in advance and the grocer despatched his son to fetch it. After they left, Ganesh withdrew a couple of hundreds from the wad he'd been given and handed these to me.

'Take Raja, Murali and Gurudas with you.' I nodded, though I felt it wasn't necessary. I could've handled it on my own. 'And come back soon; we'll celebrate in Shashikant.' We had better, I thought, considering how little I was making.

The grocer's son then went and did another stupid thing. He challenged the other lad to a rematch, and then came and told me about it.

'Eight, tonight,' he said.

'Are you sure he'll show up?'

'He'll come,' the little prick smirked. 'He thinks it's just me against him in the central garden, one-on-one.'

I would've done things differently, like having him picked up in Ganesh's van on his way to college. We could've worked him over for a couple of hours, hurting him just a bit and scaring him shitless, before letting him off with a warning. In the past we'd been through this routine a few times and it was effective. What the grocer's boy was suggesting was riskier, but also more exciting, which was why I went along with it.

At eight in the evening, Raja, Murali and I were perched on a stone bench in the main garden of Takshila, waiting for the action to begin. Gurudas had claimed an upset stomach and opted out. Pradyuman, the grocer's son, sat on a nearby bench, waiting for his rival to show up. His dad had wanted to be there as well, but I'd put my foot down on that one. I didn't plan on hurting the other guy too much, and the last thing I needed was a fool on my back demanding more bang for his buck.

It was well past the allotted hour and the lad had not shown up. We were just about to call it off when we heard the sounds.

There were at least fifteen of them, speaking in loud voices as they passed through the narrow gate of the garden in ones and twos. We realised too late that the other side had had the same idea, fighting by proxy, and, fool that I was, I hadn't even considered this.

They were on us before we had a chance to slip away, and a few of them were brandishing sticks. I was thankful for the rods we had placed under the bench, though at the time I'd considered it a bit of an overkill.

We moved towards Pradyuman, who was quaking in his sandals. The one thing he didn't know about street fights is that they can escalate like crazy.

The group was led by a huge Sikh, who appeared to be a few years older than the rest of us. I'd seen him pumping some serious iron in a gym close to where I lived. There was a gang of *Khalsas* who hung around with him, and many of these lads had turned up for the show as well.

This gent strode up to the grocer's son and landed a hard slap across his face, which deposited that worthy flat on his arse in the mud, where he remained for the duration of the fight.

It was game on, and I moved in swiftly and clipped him on the nose with a straight right. It burst open like a ripe pomegranate and began spurting blood. He moved back a few paces, roared and drew his *kirpan*.

Now this was serious business.

'*Saliya*,' I screamed at Murali, who scurried over to the bench on which we had been sitting, and within moments we, too, were armed with iron rods.

And then they charged, all in a pack. We were the interlopers, riff-raff from the *chawl*, who needed to be taught a lesson.

In no time at all I found myself in the thick of it. There were at least five guys around me, punching and slashing away. At times it appeared pretty intense, and at others it was pure vaudeville. There was a lot of wild swinging, screaming and abusing going on, most of it unnecessary. They were keeping their distance, trying to wear me down. I held them at bay for a while and then realised that more decisive action was called for. Raja was still battling on, but he wouldn't last much longer. Murali was already down and was being kicked to pieces by the big fella.

I screamed out an obscenity and lunged towards this group, targeting the huge *sardar*. He fought back gamely, slashing with his *kirpan*, and caught me on the arm. It's a scar that I carry to this day.

But by then I was on him and clunked him a good one on the noggin. The only thing that saved him was the clump of hair wound tightly inside his turban. He crashed to the ground like a felled tree and the mêlée petered out.

I was screaming like a madman, but it was mostly for appearances. Their leader was down and the rest of them just wanted to get the hell out. A couple of them were clustered around him, trying to assess just how fucked-up the situation was.

I staggered over to where Murali lay and, with Raja's assistance, helped him to his feet. His face was a mess, but at least he was walking. As we backed away through a side exit, I noticed that the grocer's boy was nowhere to be seen.

***

'What the fuck have you gone and done?' screamed Ganesh, when we landed up at the liquor *adda*.

I didn't reply. There wasn't much to say. We should've turned and fled when we had the chance.

I thought he'd ask me to go into hiding while he sorted things out. This could've posed a problem, as the only other place I could conceivably go to was my grandmother's house in Kerala.

'Go home and wait there until I send word,' he said finally. I found this odd at the time, but did as I was told.

Men of action and men of thought: it was only then that I understood the equation.

CHAPTER 6

Parry's looked like a good kid's Christmas stocking, stuffed to the brim with shiny toys and a few strange objects.

The rich prick spotted me as soon as we entered, and then his eyes turned towards Johnny Young. He was still seated at the bar counter, surrounded by his pals, but now a couple of floozies had joined them. A pair of downright uglies, I thought with satisfaction.

They were eyeing us, but warily now, wondering what I was up to. Mr Young had that effect on most people. When I looked at his arms, I understood why nations refer to their nukes as credible deterrents. You don't need to fight when you have a fella like Johnny with you; unless, of course, you want to.

We got lucky, as one of the tables freed up just as we entered. A group of kids had been waiting around for that very table, but when Mr Young strode up and plonked his buttocks on the wooden bench, nobody objected.

Ana tried protesting, but mildly. It was late and the law of the jungle ruled. We were just fortunate to have King Kong in our line-up. She and I sat down on one side of the rough wooden table, with Johnny facing us, wedged in between the sisters.

Marge's head was resting on her right arm, which lay outstretched on the table, and she seemed oblivious to the world. She'd been drinking more than all of us, and then there was the grief of the impending divorce.

The boys had begun glaring at me, and I knew they would've started something if it hadn't been for Johnny's presence. And I couldn't blame them, either. If you were young and loaded and still didn't have much luck with the ladies, I guess a bit of angst was in order.

The only problem was that this time around they were messing with the wrong fella.

***

The party was winding down, and so I decided to begin the hustle. I had to be careful, though, as Ana, I knew, would be majorly pissed off.

I picked up Marge's hand and held it in an arm-wrestling pose. She surfaced from her gloom and smiled at me. She thought I was being considerate.

I pretended to press down with all my might and she began pushing right back, and hard. She was surprisingly strong for a woman. We wrestled for a bit until Marge slammed my arm on the table. She then clasped her hands above her head and bowed to the crowd. I heard jeering from the boys at the bar, who were suddenly feeling a lot more confident.

When Johnny saw what we were doing, he wanted in on the action. We were on his turf, after all. And Jazz was not like Ana. She would in all probability just love the macho stuff.

'You arm-wrestle, maan?' Johnny asked, eyeing my wrists. At least this much he knew.

It's more of a science than one would think, is arm-wrestling. There's quite a bit of physics involved… angles, leverage, timing, and, of course, there's power. The error lies in assuming that only brute strength is enough.

'A little bit,' I said, and I knew that Ana had caught on, 'but not with guys like you.' I grinned in a self-effacing manner.

'Let's do it, maan,' he boomed.

'You'd kill me, Young,' I replied, reeling him in.

'C'mon, maan, don't be a *pussy*,' he said, and Ana gave me a nervous look.

The kids at the bar were highly energised now. They'd probably witnessed Johnny in action and wanted another show, especially against me. One by one, they slid off their bar stools and began egging the big guy on.

Johnny had his arm around Jazz's waist and was stroking the underside of her breast with his index finger. She looked like she was enjoying it.

'Go on, Vic,' Jazz urged. 'I thought you were a tough bloke, Indian Army and all.' She was mocking me, but in a flirtatious manner, which wasn't going down all that well with Ana.

'Vic, *no*,' she said, but my mind was made up.

'C'mon, soldier, don't be a pussy,' Johnny said. He had a very limited vocabulary, and if he kept this up it would get even smaller.

'I only fight for money,' I replied, and then grinned as if I was making a joke, looking for a way out. I said it loudly enough for the gang at the bar to hear, and, as expected, the rich prick finally deigned to get off his arse.

He moseyed over to our table, fished around in his cargoes and came up with a wad. It was more money than I'd ever earned in a month. This he placed in front of me.

'It's yours if you beat him,' he said, and the punks with him sniggered.

I nodded slowly, thrilled at the outcome. All I'd wanted was to rack up some betting action, but this was going way better than planned.

'If you lose, I get to dance with your girl.'

Again, I nodded. An indecent proposal, but for that much money it was only fair.

Ana didn't think so, however. She got up in a huff and went and stood at the far corner of the bar, near the pool tables. On seeing this, Marge rose from her seat and walked over to her. She was the nicer sibling, the considerate one.

Jazz was flirting with me quite openly now and this was getting Johnny all riled up. Slow he might've been, but not when it came to getting his hole.

And then Richie upped the stakes for him. He turned to the Nigerian and said, 'The money is yours if you beat him.'

Johnny looked like he'd bagged a double bonanza. If there was karaoke on, I knew which song he would've chosen, and I was grateful for that reprieve at least. As it was, my straits appeared dire enough.

The cash was on the table, as was Johnny's elbow. He was doing weird things with his bicep, which made that muscle jump about, delighting his growing band of admirers. Jazz had wriggled in closer and was running her palm over his chest. Her eyes, though, bored into mine. Maybe she knew the score, I thought. Maybe, out of all these bozos, she was the only one who knew how this would play out.

I glanced over at Ana and thought about calling the whole thing off. She sat huddled on a stool at the far end of the bar and was avoiding eye contact with me, though she knew I was looking at her. Marge had an arm around her shoulder and appeared to be explaining something to her.

I turned to face Johnny and there was a bitter taste in my mouth. I placed my elbow on the table, next to his, and he lunged for my hand. His was huge in comparison, but felt surprisingly soft. This was not a bloke who was used to doing physical work.

He was strong, though, and I knew I had to be careful. Luckily for me, he was so intent on playing to the gallery that he wasn't focusing on his grip.

The gang at the bar was crowding around us, and Johnny was showboating so much that he didn't realise what I was doing. I'd worked myself into a sweet spot where my palm was riding high up on his, and almost my entire hand was positioned against his meaty thumb.

Then I let myself go blank.

Jazz did the honours and we were pitted against one another. I was expecting the initial assault and had kept my wrist bent slightly inward to counter this.

Johnny heaved and snorted, but was unable to make much headway. Meanwhile, my fingers were working on his thumb, locking into position. When I saw disbelief replacing the earlier bravado, I moved in close and whispered, almost into his ear, 'You're going down, my friend.'

Then I waited, until he believed me, and seconds later his arm was resting on wood.

'Two out of three,' the turd said, as I pocketed his dough. His man, though, wasn't up for it. He held his forearm gingerly and pretended it was injured, and that that was the reason for his poor showing.

I rose to my feet, walked around the table and embraced Johnny. Jazz gave me a hug as well, a full frontal, but I pushed her away gently and walked over to where Ana was seated. I was feeling pretty embarrassed, which for me was uncommon. Ana had witnessed the sting once before, and she knew what had happened.

'Hey, girl,' I said, as I approached. Marge slid off her bar stool and returned to our table. She didn't acknowledge me.

'Hey,' Ana replied.

'I won,' I said, sounding silly even to myself.

'Congratulations.'

It was frosty out there in Goa.

'Is that any way to welcome your victorious soldier?' I asked. She tried to keep a straight face, but then smiled.

'And what if you had lost?' she said, when I'd taken her in my arms.

'I couldn't, *mole*. The stakes were too high.'

'Oh, what a charmer,' she said, and pinched my nose.

***

They'd started up the karaoke and the crowd was getting into the swing of things. The place was filled to bursting and we'd lost our seats. We could've got them back, courtesy of Mr Young, but I was done picking fights for the evening.

So was the big guy, apparently. He sat staring into space, like someone who has blown up his life savings. Even Jazz was ignoring him.

'Johnny,' I yelled out, 'over here, man.'

Slowly he rose from his seat, looking dazed and sheepish. Jazz and Marge followed and took up positions next to us. Jazz wedged herself into a tiny space between Johnny and me, providing both of us with an equal feel. Ana and Marge resumed from where they'd left off. I tried tuning into their conversation for a bit, but all they were doing was bashing males. Marge had had it pretty rough as far as I could make out.

'You go to a gym, maan?' asked Johnny.

'No, buddy,' I replied. 'Indian Army.'

He nodded as if he understood, but I knew that he didn't. No one could, not unless they'd been through it. During the commando course they pushed you to such extremes that it was a wonder you survived at all. Broke you into pieces, and then reassembled you in a manner they thought fit. A fighting machine without parallel, or so we were told.

Of course, I'd stopped believing in all that bullshit a long time ago.

We live in an age in which actors and sportsmen earn more in a single day than the annual pay packets of serving generals. It was enough to get you depressed. When I'd raised this point with Ana, however, she had characteristically replied, 'Why do you find it strange that people who touch so many lives, who bring so much joy to millions of folks, should be paid more than men who, essentially, are trained to kill for a living?'

And when she phrased it like that, I didn't have much of an answer. I knew, though, that there was something intrinsically wrong with the equation. Or perhaps there was only something wrong with me. Perhaps I was just another dinosaur in a fast-changing world.

***

The place was heating up and I was experiencing the glow and the abiding sense of peace that sometimes takes over when one is drinking. I had cash in my pocket and was splurging on drinks for folks I had never seen before. The guy who'd put it there had slunk out a long time ago, though a few of his cronies remained. They had come up to me, shook my hand

and clapped me on the back, and I'd ordered a round for them as well.

I turned to look at Ana, who was still tuned in to what Marge had to say. Marge was almost screaming to be heard above the din, which seemed a bit weird to me. I would've thought that when you bitch about your spouse, it ought to be done in whispers.

Her sister, though, was communicating with me in whispers. We were backed up against the bar and her index finger was making tiny whorls on my back. I was glad that Ana had her back to me and was deep in conversation with Maggie Thatcher.

Johnny, yet again, asked for and was handed the mic (his last chance of getting any, the way things were going). I could see that he was upset, but this fact seemed to have escaped Jazz; or, more likely, she just didn't give a damn.

He then proceeded to ravage three Boney M songs in a row without letting go of the mic. No one had the balls to ask for it, either. We tried singing along to *Rivers of Babylon*, but by the time Rasputin was murdered, the joint had begun to empty out.

Initially, he put his arm around Jazz and tried to drag her into the performance. I glanced at Marge, who was looking at me worriedly, but before I could intervene, Jazz had pushed his arm off and snuggled in closer to me.

Her finger had traversed the length of my spine and was doodling on the cheeks of my arse. I was sure that Marge could see what she was doing, but Jazz didn't seem unduly bothered.

'Let's go for a walk on the beach,' she whispered, her tongue brushing against my earlobe. Johnny must've noticed this, as *Daddy Cool* hit a note I'd never heard before.

'Not tonight...' I said, fobbing her off. There was a momentary gap in my liquor-induced rashness, and all I wanted was to head back to the resort with Ana.

I disengaged myself from Jazz, fingers, breast, rump *et al*, and I could make out that she was upset. I looked deep into her eyes and mouthed, 'I think you're incredible, darling, but tonight it just won't work.'

She gave me a mock pout and then winked, and we were back to being friends.

'Shall we head back?' I said to Ana, and she nodded and kissed me on the mouth.

Jazz had sidled up to the big fella and was grinding against him in tune with the music. They waved to us as we were leaving, but didn't stop the performance. *Daddy Cool* was starting to sound a whole lot better.

***

Captain Jack was perched on a sofa in the lobby of his resort. He was staring at a muted TV screen and sipping from a glass of *feni*. The drink, which had made him so affable just a while earlier, had by now turned him into a zombie.

'Hi, Uncle Jack,' Ana shouted, chirpy as ever, no small thanks to the PCs she'd been imbibing. The geezer glanced at us briefly, before turning back to his television.

We reached our cottage, let ourselves in and collapsed on the bed.

The idea of making love several times a day is far more gratifying than the real thing, but we went through the motions anyway. Ana dropped off immediately after (or perhaps even during; I couldn't really say) and I lay beside her on the dank mattress and stared up at the ceiling.

Sleep wouldn't come, however, nor would the thoughts subside… about my father, Amritsar, my abeyant writing career, and the general rut my life had slithered into.

I thought about sneaking out to a bar and then decided that the lobby was better.

Captain Jack was sprawled out on the sofa now, still cradling his precious glass. He showed no signs of turning in, which was not surprising given what awaited him. I asked for and was provided a drink, grudgingly this time around, and we both gazed at the tube in silence while sipping from our glasses.

CHAPTER 7

It was past midnight when they came for me.

There were two of them, skinny little runts wearing khaki shorts and *topis*, and they began pounding on our door repeatedly. Luckily for me, the chump was so far gone that he barely registered what was happening. I considered slipping out through a back window, but that would only delay the inevitable, and besides, Ganesh had sort of hinted that he would take care of things.

I slid open the latch and stepped out, and they didn't even bother to slap me around. They might've wanted to, but I already looked pretty messed up.

I'd taken a glance at the mirror and what I saw startled me. One eye was rimmed with flecks of red which had begun to turn black. The other was pulpy and tightly shut. I had wrapped a towel around the cut on my arm, but blood was seeping through. My chest and neck were badly scratched and there was a deep bite mark on my thumb. All in all, quite a shitty state to be in.

I'd expected a police van, or at least a jeep, but there was only a rickshaw waiting (I guess I didn't rank very high in the criminal stakes). I was placed in between the duo, and in that cramped, bouncy position was carted off to the cop station in MIDC.

I think they felt a bit bad on seeing my condition (though, being macho males in an uber-macho profession, they tried not to show it). Added to this was the fact that I didn't look like your average miscreant, and for this I had to be thankful for my Anglo lineage. God knows, if it got me out of this mess, I'd be grateful to Grandpa Samson for the first time ever.

They made me wait on a bench for a long time, which was fine by me. I figured this meant that I wasn't going to be locked up any time soon, but I was mistaken. Raja was dragged in a few hours later and then both of us were escorted to a cell.

Raja informed me that Murali was in hospital with a shattered kneecap, and the initial prognosis (which turned out to be correct) was that he would always walk with a limp. The other guy, the huge *sardar* I'd clobbered, had been admitted to the very same hospital, and it was his father who had lodged the complaint. The guy was related to a senior cop and he was out to get me. The blood seeping out of my left arm just wasn't enough.

Things were starting to look grim in that dingy cell, but I was still hopeful that Ganesh would deliver.

***

Around four in the morning, just as we had begun to drop off, we were taken for a round of "questioning"; Raja first, and then yours truly.

They led me to a largish room at the back, which was illuminated by a single light bulb. There were three men inside, two of whom had stripped down to their undershirts. One of them was breathing heavily and held an unfamiliar implement in his hand.

It was a wooden baton, to which was attached a thick leather strap. I found out a bit later that this was dipped in oil periodically to prevent skin from breaking.

'*Achcha*, so this is our local Rocky,' the other one said, and I made the mistake of smiling at him. The strap caught me across the face, and I let out a yelp and backed up against a wall.

'Wait,' the third cop said; an inspector, by the looks of it. 'Strip down to your underwear.' He was perched on a stool and had a detached air about him, as though he was watching his wife's favourite soap on television.

I did as I was told. It wasn't a request, anyway.

The blows began raining down on me as I crouched in a corner trying not to scream. Each time I bunched myself into a ball to present a smaller target, the constables would begin kicking me. The gash on my arm had opened up and droplets of blood were splattered all over the cell.

'His condition was recorded when he was brought in, right?' the inspector enquired at one point.

'Yes, sir,' a constable replied. They needn't have been concerned, though. In our world, lodging a complaint against a cop was a potential death sentence.

The beating went on for a long time, or at least it seemed that way to me. When they reckoned that I'd had enough, the inspector spoke.

'Bring him to my room,' he said, and walked out.

I was told to stand up, but found that I couldn't. I really wanted to, just to prove a point, but my legs had turned to jelly. It wasn't so much the strap as it was the kicks to my thighs and kidneys. I rose to my feet once, but couldn't stay upright and plonked down on my arse, legs splayed out in front of me.

It was embarrassing, and the *pandus*, not surprisingly, found it incredibly funny.

'Remember this the next time you think about creating work for us,' one said to me, as they dragged me to their boss's cabin.

'Careful… you're hurting me,' I whined, and we all had a laugh. They weren't such bad blokes after all. And if there was no filth in the world, you wouldn't need brutes like these to clean it up.

'What is your name?' the inspector asked.

'Victor, sir. Victor Gabriel.'

'Victor Gabriel,' he repeated slowly. 'Are you a *gora*?'

'My father's an Anglo-Indian, sir.'

We were all alone in his cabin. He didn't consider me to be much of a threat, evidently.

'Ganesh Mhatre asked you to do this, right?'

I stared at a paperweight on his desk.

'There's no point in denying it. We've picked up Pradyuman, and his father as well. They've already confessed to everything.'

Still I said nothing.

'You know that boy with you, Rajaram, he claims that it was all your idea, that all he and his friend were trying to do was stop the fight.'

Yeah, sure, I thought, but there was no point in saying anything.

'You don't believe me, do you? Why don't you ask him yourself?'

They led me back to the holding cell and I did ask Raja. He appeared furtive and embarrassed, and I knew that what the cop had told me was true.

To be fair, they had worked him over quite badly, much more than they'd done to me. He could not even take a few steps without stumbling. I hadn't known this, but Raja was a habitual offender, a *dus numbri*. He had to come in every week and sign in a register kept in the inspector's office. I didn't blame him for selling me out; well, not too much, anyway.

***

The next morning, my dad showed up at the cop station and they brought me out to meet him.

'They haven't charged you yet, *mone*,' he informed me. 'I'm trying to get you out before they file a FIR.' For once, our roles were reversed, and it was I who felt mortified by what I'd done.

Pradyuman was hauled in the next morning and remained inside for a day before being released. I saw the big *sardar* in the cop station, too, looking very nervous. He was accompanied by some formidable *Khalsas*, but all of them appeared to be intimidated by the slender, neat-looking inspector.

No one was booked, however. I found out later that some serious money had changed hands. Pradyuman's dad had shelled out the most. He was forced to sell his grocery store a few months later to pay off his debts. Ganesh had had to cough up a packet as well, and call in all his favours. The *sardar*'s family was not spared either, plus he had a dent in his noggin to boot.

Raja and I had nothing to offer, and so we remained in the lock-up until things were settled, and the cops were convinced that neither side would be levelling allegations or pressing charges.

I was inside for almost a week and the inspector had begun to take an interest in me.

The beatings had stopped after the second day, and then one evening I was escorted to his cabin so that he could have a chat with me.

'I hope that from now on you're going to stay away from Ganesh,' he began.

'I will, sir,' I replied, and meant it.

'They're in a lot of trouble as it is, and they will drag you down with them. I've seen it happen to many boys from good families.'

I stared at my feet.

'After you get out, if you face any trouble from them, come and see me, and I'll take care of it.'

I nodded.

'Do you know that your father has been coming here every single day to try to persuade me not to register a case against you?' This caught me by surprise. My dad had shown up at the station the morning after the incident, but I'd assumed it was because he'd been summoned by the police.

'And do you know what he offered me? Your room in the *chawl* if I could get you out.'

I stared at the paperweight, which was turning blurry.

'He's a good man, son; an alcoholic, but still a good man. He told me what happened with your mother.'

I was crying now, appalled at myself, but unable to stop.

'Yesterday, he came here with the principal of Dominic Savio. They tell me that you're a sportsman, and that you captained their football team.'

I nodded.

'I'm going to try my best to get you out of this, but if you ever come back, I will make sure you regret it. Do you understand?' he said with a burst of ferocity.

Once again, I nodded.

'I've been watching you, son. You're intelligent and strong, and very brave. These are qualities you should use to go ahead. Choose a career in which these will come in handy. Study hard, and then join the police force, or the army, or something like that. Try and make a contribution to society. You have only one life — don't throw it away.'

CHAPTER 8

I woke up at six as I usually did, even though I'd fallen asleep only a few hours earlier. Jack had still been at it when I'd crawled back to our room, done with both his *feni* and his company.

Ana showed no signs of getting up, and so I hung around in the room and tried my hand at writing.

I always carried a notebook on me, a habit from my schooldays, but this one had barely been used. Just doodles of oversized breasts and penises on the first page and fuckfuckfuckfuckfuck scrawled all over the second, which didn't make for either great art or literature.

Despite this, I forced myself to sit at the desk, pen clutched resolutely in hand. A few months earlier a germ of an idea had washed up against me, about a good-natured hustler in the heart of Bombay's red-light district. It'd seemed quite appealing at the time, and I'd bounced it around in my head for a while. But, as is often the case, when it finally took shape on paper it read like trash: lifeless and two-dimensional. I had already mutilated one draft, and this was going to be my attempt at a second.

I sat hunched over the desk for an eternity, but the pen refused to budge. I even picked up the copy of the New Testament and leafed through this for inspiration. A little leaven leaveneth the whole lump, it said, confounding me further.

'You're *writing*!' squealed Ana. 'I'm so, so glad.'

I was too: that I had my back towards her. I shut the notebook with a flourish, stood up and faced her.

'Aren't you at least going to show me what you've written?' she asked.

'When it's done,' I replied mysteriously.

'And where were you last night? I heard you going out.'

'Uncle Jack was feeling frisky. I thought he could use some company.'

Ana giggled. 'How considerate. Are you sure you didn't sneak back to Parry's? Jazz was quite smitten, y'know.'

I hooted, as if the mere idea was preposterous.

'With me, or Mr Young?'

'Both of you, I think... it would make for quite a threesome.'

'So, what do you want to do today?' I asked, and saw her perking up. Holidays with me usually meant counting steps to the nearest bar.

'I thought we could hire a taxi for the day and head south. Maybe drive around Panjim for a while.'

'Sure,' I said. After the previous night's performance, I owed her at least that much.

***

We bathed together, lathering each other to wonderful climaxes, and then headed to the restaurant for breakfast. I'd skipped dinner altogether and was feeling pretty famished.

The Braganzas were seated at one of the tables, and Uncle Jack (a far better man when the missus wasn't around) was giving me the cold shoulder.

Miranda, too, was as surly as ever. I could sense that she felt I was not good enough for Ana, and for this I couldn't fault her. A lot of folks felt exactly the same way.

'*Good* morning, Aunty, good morning, Uncle Jack,' Ana chirped like a pre-schooler.

'You slept well, or what?' This from the captain, who hadn't bothered to acknowledge *moi*, his first mate and drinking buddy.

'Yes, Uncle, very well, but Victor tells me that both you rascals were up late drinking. Very, very naughty,' she tut-tutted, nodding her head from side to side.

I watched the crone's eyebrows converging and Jack's face losing colour. I guess doling out free drinks when she was not around was not considered kosher.

'We're thinking of driving down to Panjim,' I put in, trying to change the subject.

'Wow,' said Jack listlessly.

'What do you suggest we do there?' asked Ana.

'Look in a guidebook,' he muttered, and Ana held on tightly to my arm.

We filled our plates at the buffet counter and sat as far away from them as possible.

'What did you say to him last night?' asked Ana. She wasn't used to being treated with disrespect, and it was bothering her.

'Nothing,' I replied. 'I gave him some tips on how to perk up his sex life.'

'What tips?'

'I told him that he could start by divorcing his wife.'

She giggled.

'No wonder he doesn't seem to like you.'

'Right now, my love, I don't think he likes *you* very much, either.'

We burst out laughing and I noticed the old folks staring at us. The crone had a vicious expression on her mug, which didn't make her any prettier.

***

It was past ten in the morning when we stepped out and my stomach was already feeling queasy. All thoughts of making the day memorable for Ana had taken a backseat. What I craved was a drink, and badly.

'Where are we going, Vic?' she asked, as I dragged her past the taxi stand.

'One drink, sweetheart, just one for the road, I promise,' I replied.

She snatched away her hand from mine, but didn't say anything. The Ana of old would've stormed off on her own to Panjim, and not spoken to me for a week. She was really giving this a shot, I thought despondently.

I wanted to be done with it quickly, and so we stepped into the very first bar we came across. It was a grungy little dive, right on the main street, littered with a couple of semi-corpses, who were not there for the ambience, and didn't add to it either.

Time to lighten the mood, I thought, else it could turn into a killer of a day.

'You see that guy over there?' I said, pointing to a bozo clad in ragged Bermudas and a greasy fishnet vest.

'What about him?' she replied, feigning disinterest.

'He's the head of the Russian mob. They're moving all their operations to Goa.'

'The *bossman*?' Ana asked, eyes twinkling. Finally.

I nodded. 'The top guy.'

'Times seem to be tough in Mother Russia,' she said, and both of us burst out laughing. It was what I liked most about her. She could never hold a grudge for too long.

My drink took forever to arrive, even though there were only two other customers in the bar. This was par for the course in Goa, especially if you were brown-skinned. I took a gulp from the glass dumped in front of me and moments later my world began to perk up. Ana had refused to order anything, and appeared quite tetchy. I took my time, however. It was my first drink of the day and needed to be savoured.

The mob boss glanced our way and did a double-take when he saw Ana. He then looked at me, grinned and turned away. I knew he was bouncing topics around in his head, waiting to strike up a conversation. I also knew that being a *gora*, his opening line would be about the weather.

'Whoa,' he said finally, turning fully around and facing us, 'it sure gets sweaty around here after the monsoons.'

I smiled in encouragement, but Ana, surprisingly, ignored him. I guess she wanted to hit the road as quickly as possible; not stay and indulge in small talk with a Russian mobster, who, when we got to know him better, would most likely mutate into a middle-aged English wino.

I gave him another smile, this time the nasty one, and he turned away. A fair-weather friend, I thought, mentally patting myself at my own witticism.

'*C'mon*, Vic, get a move on. I don't want to sit here all day.'

'Hey, look who's here,' I said, and Ana turned to see. It was the hairdressing duo from Manchester.

They were waddling towards us, all oiled up, and looking like moving masses of broiled meat. Even Jazz, who I thought came across as really sexy the night before, was a let-down the day after.

'*Marge*,' Ana squealed, and I was genuinely pleased. I could sure use the company.

'Hi, Ana,' Marge replied, just as enthusiastically. Jazz, though, was squirming, less than thrilled to be spotted in her current state. Ana asked them to join us, but they appeared a bit hesitant, until I rose from my seat and shepherded them into the bar.

'So, what time did you guys wind up last night?' I asked, staring at a hickey on Jazz's neck.

'Soon after you folks left,' Marge replied.

'Johnny wanted to take us to some club he manages called Black Out, but both of us were knackered. Headed straight back to our rooms,' Jazz added.

Sure, I thought, and he sent you the love bite by courier. I ordered pina coladas for them and another *feni* for me.

'So, what do you folks plan to do today?' Marge asked.

'We're going to spend the day in Panjim,' Ana replied.

'Why don't you join us?' I put in, and saw Jazz's eyes lighting up.

'Of course not,' Marge replied. 'You lovebirds ought to be on your own.'

'Nonsense! We insist. It'll be fun,' I said, not looking at Ana.

The sisters exchanged glances, but it really was a no-brainer. Plan B was getting fried on the beach.

'Are you *sure*?' Marge asked in her schoolmarm-ish tone, and it was beginning to get a tad irritating. What did she expect us to say... that we'd changed our minds and didn't want them tagging along?

'Of course, Marge, please join us. It'll be wonderful to have you along,' Ana replied, a bit stiffly, I thought.

'All right then,' Marge said. 'Will you give us ten minutes? We'll get changed and be back in a jiffy.'

CHAPTER 9

Ten minutes turned out to be half an hour, during which time Ana and I barely spoke to each other.

'What's the matter?' I asked, feigning ignorance. 'Didn't you want them to tag along?'

'It's fine,' she replied.

'I only asked because I thought you'd want Marge to join us.'

'So very considerate of you.'

'If you're going to be this way about it, I'll just pop by their hotel and inform them that we've changed our minds... that we'd prefer to be alone.'

'Oh, so now you know where they're staying?'

'They told us last night, Ana. C'mon, you were there, too.'

'I said it was okay, Vic,' she replied, and I let the matter drop.

Luckily for me, the sisters showed up shortly thereafter. Marge looked about the same, though she did have more clothes on, but Jazz... now that babe had really dolled up. She was wearing a plunging yellow top with a lot of cleavage showing, and an emerald green sarong.

'She's certainly gone to some trouble for you,' Ana murmured, and I laughed, perhaps a bit louder than was warranted.

'Hey, folks, we're ready,' Jazz said breezily. 'Shall we head out?'

I suggested a last round, for the road and all, but the ladies were reluctant, and so we began walking towards the taxi stand.

Uncle Joe was loitering around there, and he leapt out of his cab when he saw us approaching. Ana appeared delighted to see *him*.

'What's up, men? Where you off to?' he asked.

'Panjim, but first we want to make a detour to Anjuna.'

'*I'll* take you, men... cheap,' he said, and I snorted. I was yet to find a cheap taxi in Goa.

I took the little guy aside and commenced the negotiation. He, of course, would have preferred to have this talk with Ana, but the lady in question was engaged in an animated conversation with the hairdressers, about important things like face creams, hair gels and that kind of stuff.

When we were done, and Uncle Joe looked a lot less happy than before, I summoned the ladies over.

'Okay, girls, this is the plan... first we head to Anjuna for some bargain shopping, and then we drive out to Panjim for lunch and sightseeing.'

The sisters seemed pretty excited, and even Ana perked up on hearing the plan. She knew just how much I hated shopping. I would need to steer them away from the shops quickly, though, or else it would be a long day for me.

***

The road to Anjuna was lousy, but the surrounding countryside was breath-taking. It was decked out in shades of green so vibrant that it almost hurt the eyes. To me it felt like being ensconced in the cupped palms of the Almighty.

Like the Himalayas, I thought, and parts of Punjab in the early morning, and then I willed myself to think of other things before the memories took hold of me.

'Joe, you have some more of that *feni* on you?'

'No,' he replied in a terse manner, clearly miffed with me. I didn't feel sorry for him, however. Just the tip that Ana had given him the previous day would have paid for this trip twice over.

We pulled up at a parking spot near the Anjuna market and headed towards the stalls. Right on cue, we were assailed by a horde of urchins, mostly girls, offering us an assortment of wares that I for one had no intention of purchasing.

Ana and the sisters immersed themselves in the goods on offer and I informed them that I would catch up with them later. I'd fought a war in Punjab, an insidious one, and gone through commando training, but shopping was an ordeal I couldn't stomach.

I headed to a nearby bar (which, thankfully, is never hard to find in this part of the world) and ordered my fourth drink of the morning. It was approaching mid-day by then, which made it about par for the course.

Uncle Joe was strolling around the marketplace and I called him over for a drink. It was going to be a long day, I knew, and the last thing I needed was a surly companion.

The girls were done earlier than I'd expected, with Joe and I still midway through our second round. They joined us at the table and I ordered drinks for everyone. Ana seemed happy enough, and I heaved a secret sigh of relief.

They laid out their booty on the table, which included hairclips and scarves and odd-looking bead necklaces that I knew Ana for one would never be wearing. Her tastes were quite contradictory that way. She enjoyed slumming, and mingling with the hoi polloi, but decked out in Gucci and Versace.

Ana and Marge sat facing each other and were indulging in a heart-to-heart which had spilled over from the night before. Jazz was seated in front of me and accidentally-on-purpose her feet were pressed up against mine. Every once in a while, she would stroke my foot with her big toe. It was quite stimulating to say the least, and both of us were only half-tuned into Joe's prattle.

**

We were just about ready to hit the road when a girl of perhaps ten walked up to our table. She was holding up a bundle of brightly-coloured sarongs.

'*Bonjour, mesdames*,' she said with barely an accent, and I could see that the sisters were pretty chuffed, being mistaken for Frenchies and all.

'We're English, luv,' Marge said, and Jazz guffawed.

'What's *your* name?' asked Ana.

'My name is Radha,' she replied in schoolgirl English.

'Where are you from?'

'Karnataka.'

'Where in Karnataka?' Ana persisted.

'Hassan,' the kid replied, mentioning the name of a town not too far from Bangalore. Anjuna was a long way from home. 'You buy these?'

'How much?' Jazz asked.

'Normal price is four hundred rupees, but for you, special rate, only three hundred.'

Both Jazz and Marge snorted in unison, which I guess was the recommended response in the travel guides they were consulting.

'Thirty,' Marge said, and Jazz rolled her eyes at her, as if offering a tenth of the asking rate was still way too much. The kid whined and pleaded for a long time before dropping the price to a hundred rupees.

'Final,' she said, and looked as if she meant it.

'Ninety,' said Jazz, and looked as if she meant it, too.

They argued for almost ten minutes before settling on ninety-five. I did the maths in my head and knew that if Jazz had chanced upon the equivalent of five rupees on a sidewalk in Manchester, she wouldn't have stuck out her butt to pick it up.

Marge had an approving smile on her face, while the rest of us were squirming.

Drinks over, we rose to leave. The sisters walked on ahead with Joe and we followed some distance behind. Ana gestured to Radha to come over and slipped her a note, and the smile we received was worth more than all her sarongs put together.
I pulled Ana close and kissed her, and she linked her arms around my waist as we headed to the taxi.

CHAPTER 10

Ana and I hooked up a year or so after I left the army.

In the outside world, I soon found out that jobs for ex-*faujis* were in short supply. All too often, the best you could hope for was to head up security in a large corporation, and be treated like a fond relic by prepubescent pups with MBAs, whose bonuses were several times your annual pay packet.

Not that I was looking for a high-paying job or anything. I'd already decided that I wanted to be a writer, which meant that the most I could realistically aspire to was somewhere in between a living wage and starvation.

I penned my first short story when I was nineteen, while still at the NDA, and after much deliberation, I sent it out to a magazine. Afterwards I forgot about it completely, until a few months later, when I received a letter in the post (with a cheque enclosed) informing me that my story had been accepted. I still have a copy of that mag lying around somewhere.

What I was looking for was something in journalism, which I reasoned would be the right step in my literary career. One thing I was clear about —

I would not write about my experiences in the army. To do so would require that I sift through layers of shit that were best left undisturbed.

I applied to a host of magazines and newspapers, first the serious ones like *India Today* and the *Express*, and then, when no responses were forthcoming, to several others. Initially, I'd resolved not to mention my *fauji* background, but then, when even negative replies stopped coming, I sent in fresh résumés that included my army experience.

After that, I received an answer to almost every application I sent out. The responses, though, were still the same — negative. There just weren't any vacancies available, I was informed, but they would get in touch as soon as there were.

I even applied to the film glossies, I was that desperate.

***

Finally, I decided to settle for a lower rung on the wordsmith's ladder, and here I met with some success.

I sent in my résumé to a number of ad agencies, and was thrilled when almost immediately I landed a job interview. It was a smallish agency, tucked away in a by-lane in the Fort area, and I arrived a bit late, as I had trouble locating the place.

The interview had been scheduled for nine in the morning, but even at ten I was the only one there aside from the office boy who had let me in. This was another thing I was figuring out about civilian life. What would've been deemed a hanging offence in the Services was par for the course on the outside.

The agency was owned by a couple of Sindhi businessmen, but was run by a *pattar* from Palghat named Venu Aiyar. He ambled in at eleven, which I later found out was early by his standards. Apparently, he had a lengthy list of spiritual tasks to conclude before commencing work.

'You were in the army or what?' he began, after scanning through my résumé.

'Yes, sir.'

'Which regiment?'

'I was in the Rifles, sir, posted in Punjab.'

'Hmmm,' he murmured, 'I have a friend in the army, Bhaskaran Pillai. Do you know him?'

'No, sir,' I replied. There are over a million soldiers in the Indian Army, you idiot, I thought charitably.

'Have you seen any action?' he went on. The one topic that guarantees any *fauji* an audience.

'Yes, sir,' I replied, dreading what was to follow.

'Have you killed anyone?'

I paused before answering, 'Yes, sir, but I don't want to talk about it.'

He nodded. 'When can you start?'

'Sir?' I gulped.

'You came here for a job interview, son. So, when can you start work?'

'Today, sir,' I replied, my heart leaping.

'No... not today... join from tomorrow,' he muttered absent-mindedly. The meeting was over as far as he was concerned. I shook his hand and rose to leave.

'Just one more thing, son: you'll be expected to join me for client meetings, so try and dress a bit better.' This from a chappie who had a quart of *sambar* from his breakfast splattered all over his shirt.

'Yes, sir.' I said.

CHAPTER 11

And that was how I started out as a copywriter in Amadeus Inc., which, when you think about it, was a pretty highfalutin name for a shithole of a place. Thankfully, however, the Sindhi bosses had refrained from calling it G&W (Gurbaxani and Wadhwani), which was the trend in those days.

I spent almost a year in the Bombay office, doing grunt work like the copy you see on bottles of cough syrup and floor cleaner, and it wasn't as if anyone (except for my dad) even read the stuff I wrote.

Naturally, the constellation of stars in the agency would never get involved in such piddling jobs. The creative director and supervisor spent most of their time ideating, which was their term of choice for lighting up joints and bullshitting about life in general. Even the owners got into the vibe whenever they deigned to visit. One of them sported a ratty ponytail and this bozo would pop into the conference room every so often for a drag. I think it upped his coolness quotient, the hanging out with creative folk and playing at adman (while taking a well-deserved break from his daily routine of hawking toilet fittings).

With the exception of Aiyar, I couldn't stand the lot, but I did my best to stay out of trouble. Until, that is, the creative head, Ajay Sippy, no doubt taken in by my meek demeanour, began getting on my tits.

He started out by making digs at army men in general and me in particular. I think he wished to project himself as a left-of-centre, pot-imbibing peacenik, which was fine with me as long as he didn't squeeze *my* nuts. But he did, repeatedly, and since I didn't react at first, it only encouraged him to keep at it.

Until, that is, I talked him out of it.

***

The turd was leaning against a wall in the hallway outside our office when he spotted me trudging up the stairwell. The office was on the seventh floor, but I preferred to leg it, as the elevator was one of those rickety, caged contraptions that sometimes stopped on its own volition between levels.

He was chatting up one of the interns and my arrival on the scene offered some scope for comic relief, or so he figured.

'Hey, Victor, this building has a lift, you know,' he said.

'So?'

'Is it like an army thing? You soldier-boys just don't *like* using all these modern amenities?'

'It's a fitness thing, buddy. I for one like being able to see what's hanging below, which, I'm guessing, doesn't matter all that much to you,' I replied, pointing to his midriff. He was slender in most aspects, but had a gut that hung over his belt like a large tumour. The loose *kurtas* he favoured weren't merely a style statement.

The girl was giggling, and I grinned at her. She was definitely one of the prettier faces in the office.

'Oh, you think that's funny, arsehole?' he asked angrily, pulling rank just like in the army. Only this wasn't the army. I reached out and grabbed hold of his throat.

'Who did you call an arsehole, fucker?' I said.

He looked into my eyes and quickly realised his error. But the intern was standing right there and so he couldn't let it drop, either.

'Let go of me,' he croaked. 'Sak… Sakshi, go and inform Mr Aiyar.' But Sakshi wasn't going anywhere. This was as much action as she'd seen in a week with us, and she wouldn't miss a minute of it.

I pushed the chump up against the wall.

'Listen, buddy, let me explain something to you,' I said. 'I came here to do a job and I'm trying to do it as best as I can. You want to play the office comedian, go and do it someplace else. You understand?'

He nodded.

When I moved my hand away, I saw that his throat had turned an interesting shade of pink. He looked ready to cry as he slunk into the office, shoulders drooping, tits resting on the aforementioned gut.

Sakshi was grinning at me.

'Do me a favour, luv,' I said, 'don't mention this to anyone, okay? Both of us need to continue working here.'

'Sure,' she said glibly, and I knew it would be all over the office by lunchtime.

'You fancy going out for a coffee some time?' I asked.

'Yup,' she replied. 'Call me, whenever.'

***

Aiyar took a whole week to bring it up, during which time I naively presumed that the incident had been buried and forgotten. But that wasn't the way things worked, however.

When the call finally came, it was all very official. Aiyar's secretary buzzed to inform me that he wished to see me at six sharp, just before closing time. The man sat in a glass-enclosed cabin not ten feet away, and could've summoned me by crooking his finger. But no, things had to be done in a certain way.

'Ajay claims that you assaulted him,' Aiyar began, as soon as I'd pushed open the door of his cabin. I could make out that he was nervous and trying to conceal this beneath a veneer of aggression.

'He said that, did he?'

'What really happened, according to you?'

'It's true... in a sense. One could presume that I assaulted him.'

'*Why*?' It was a good question, the logical one, but I didn't feel like explaining. I'd already packed my stuff and was ready to move out.

'There was another person who was present at the time. Did you check with her?'

'Yes,' he replied, gazing forlornly at a *sambhar* stain on his shirt.

'And...?'

'She told me that he provoked you, that he used abusive language.'

'Well, then,' I said.

'It's not that simple, Victor. The guy happens to be Gurbax's nephew.' Gurbax, aka Mohan Gurbaxani, the dick with the ponytail.

'You know I like you, Victor, and you've been doing some good work of late. But he has already complained to his uncle.' That was one nice thing about the Indian Army, I thought. There weren't too many uncles floating around, pissing down on people's careers. You pretty much needed to fuck it up all on your own, as I'd succeeded in doing.

'Tell me what you want me to do, sir. I'm okay with anything you decide.'

He paused before replying.

'Could you relocate to Bangalore?'

'Why?' I asked.

'I've convinced them to let me transfer you.'

'What's in Bangalore?'

'We've just set up shop there. It's a tiny operation, but they could use a copywriter.'

I mulled over the offer for barely a second.

'Okay,' I replied, and watched his face light up.

I didn't care that much for this rathole anyway.

CHAPTER 12

Bangalore was surprisingly warm when I arrived there in mid-October. Folks in the Bombay office had briefed me on the weather, how I needed to pack plenty of woollens for the cold spells in winter; but the place was sweltering when I got there.

It was easy to fit in, though. Rents were low, the commute almost non-existent, and working hours shorter. I moved into PG digs near Ulsoor Lake, close to where my office was located, and from where I could walk to work. This, for me, was a huge upgrade after the hour-long brawls in Bombay locals.

The office, though, was a let-down. We were considered a small agency in Bombay, a boutique firm focused on cutting-edge creative (as we plugged ourselves to clients), but here we were miniscule, almost insignificant.

There were only three of us in the Bangalore branch — a guy from Coorg named Cariappa, who serviced our few accounts; an office peon whose name I've forgotten; and yours truly, the in-house creative talent.

Cariappa, or Carey as he liked to call himself, had been doubling up as creative head before I arrived on the scene, a fact that he never let me forget.

At first, Curry (I preferred to call him that, though he asked me more than once not to) perceived me as a threat, having been sent from HO and all; but after he had spent some time in my company, he stopped worrying.

As far as I was concerned, I was simply biding my time, trying to accumulate life experiences that I could turn into a book. It was hard, though, as corporate life was a real drag after my stint in the army.

Bangalore, however, was a breath of fresh air. The climate eventually did get cooler, and, on the other hand, Curry began warming up to me. Initially, he tried to stick his nose in my work, but after our boundaries were more clearly defined (I had to tell him to fuck off a few times), things turned out quite well for both of us.

Curry had a quasi-cultured air about him, which he could tap into at will, and he was also adept at working the party circuit. Both these talents brought in just enough business to keep us afloat. Since there was little work and loads of free time, I took to going on long walks around the city. Creative leeway ensured that I was not pulled up for this. Besides, I was not averse to sitting late in the office on occasion, something that Curry was loath to do.

***

It was on one of these outings that it happened.

I used to frequent a bookstore located off MG Road that served the most amazing filter coffee. Also, there were chairs and sofas strewn around the place, and they didn't mind folks perusing the books on offer. This was a huge draw for me, given my compulsive need to read, and the nature of my finances.

One afternoon, I was combing through the shelves for something affordable when I spotted her hunched over on a stool in the Classics section.

She looked up, caught me staring at her, gave me a smile and went back to her reading.

And precisely at that moment, your hero was totally smitten.

To say that she was good-looking was an understatement. Her features were exquisite and her eyes seemed almost luminescent. Her smile, though fleeting, was friendly, and drew me in like a magnet. I knew she was way out of my league, but I also knew that I just *had* to initiate a conversation.

'This one's okay,' I said, 'but you should read his short stories. They're way better.' She was holding a copy of *For Whom the Bell Tolls*.

She raised her head and smiled at me, and I knew I would remember the moment forever. Suddenly, I felt conscious about my frayed jeans and sandals.

'Which book would you recommend?' she asked. I wondered whether she was mocking me, but her expression was guileless.

'You could try *The First Forty-Nine Stories*... over there,' I said, pointing. 'My personal favourite is one called *The Snows of Kilimanjaro*.'

'I've read that,' she said, 'and I *loved* it. There's a line in the story which goes something like "The rich are not different... they are dull and repetitious." It's true, you know.'

I didn't know any rich folks, but I took her word for it.

'Thanks for the suggestion... and happy reading.' She smiled again and went back to her novel. My heart felt like it had been wrenched from its moorings.

But that was it for me. There was only so much pluck that one could summon up. I scanned through the Classics, pulled out a Steinbeck, and slunk off to the coffee counter. Payday was a few weeks away, but browsing was free.

I settled into an armchair and began reading. I liked Steinbeck a lot, almost as much as Hemingway. I liked his take on the little guy, and his quasi-commie perspective. I loved the way his characters battled against insurmountable odds, and did not always come out triumphant. This was a man who had possessed both the magic and the craft, and I would have lopped off my thumb to write like him.

'I bought the book you recommended,' she said, as she pulled up a chair and sat down next to me.

I gazed at her, flabbergasted. Up close, she was even more attractive, especially when she smiled.

'My name's Ana,' she said, holding out her hand.

'Victor,' I croaked. 'Can I get you a coffee?'

'I've already ordered. Vikas will be bringing it.'

'I thought you had already read it,' I said, pointing to the book in her hand.

'Just a few of the stories, in another collection; but there are some here I haven't read.'

'I didn't know girls liked Hemingway,' I said. It was a struggle to keep the conversation going, and I was also weighed down by the state of my attire.

I found out later that these were precisely the factors that had drawn her to me. Plus, my misshapen snout, which she claimed she found "interesting".

'That's typical male stereotyping,' she teased. 'Why can't women like Hemingway?'

I grinned. I liked her even more now.

'He writes for men, mostly,' I replied. 'They say he even preferred men, towards the end.'

'Oh, you have something against gay folks too?' she asked, her eyes twinkling.

'No,' I said, 'only happy ones.'

She laughed then, and it was a fine laugh, loud and unbridled, and completely at odds with her appearance.

We chatted for over an hour, and by the time I rose to leave she'd invited me out for dinner.

CHAPTER 13

I was starting to worry about Uncle Joe. A pint bottle of *feni* had magically appeared and he and I were sipping from this in turns. We were back in his rattletrap, on our way to Panjim, and I could see that the pressure of being tour guide and chief entertainer (combined with his habitual role of career drunk) was beginning to tell on him. The *feni* by itself he could handle, but the *feni* coupled with all the female attention was getting to him. Every once in a while, in mid-conversation, the car would veer off at a diagonal until one of the ladies squealed and tapped him on the shoulder. It would then straighten course for a bit, before going off track again.

After a while of this, I instructed him to pull over. He appeared a bit flustered when I asked for the keys, but didn't protest too much. I got behind the wheel and things improved somewhat. The ladies settled down as Joe waxed eloquent about Goan history (or at least one version thereof). My driving was only marginally better, but at least I was sticking to a straight line.

'So where do you girls want to go first?' I asked.

'Vic, can we stop at Bom Jesus?' said Ana.

I wasn't much of a church-goer, but I noticed both sisters nodding excitedly.

'Sure,' I replied, and took the left towards Old Goa.

The road was in a pathetic state and it took us almost half-an-hour to get there. We left the cab in the car park and walked towards the monument.

'Aren't you coming?' Jazz asked.

'I'll wait here. You folks have fun,' I replied.

'How come?' said Marge. 'Aren't you Catholic?'

'Lapsed,' I smiled. 'It's what happens when you have religion beaten into you at an early age.'

Which wasn't true of course, just writer's blarney. The only thing my dad was religious about came in glass bottles.

I squatted in the shade of a tree, Joe's *feni* bottle in hand, and sipped from this intermittently. The gent in question, in an admirable display of chivalry, had insisted on accompanying the womenfolk to church.

I was thinking about Ammama, who I hadn't spoken to in years. When she was around, she would insist that I accompany her to mass on Sundays, but after she left, I stopped going altogether.

I sat there for a while, slugging from the bottle, but the mugginess and the memories began to bother me, and so I put the pint in my pocket and went into the church. It was definitely cooler inside.

***

There's something very soothing about empty churches. This one was ancient, and contained the body of a Christian saint, which had not decomposed even after almost five centuries. I'd read a story about a Portuguese noblewoman who had bitten off the saint's toe when his remains were placed on display. The incident had taken place in the sixteenth century, though tour guides in Goa made it sound as if it had occurred just the previous week.

The ladies were seated in the front pews, a little apart from each other. Marge seemed frail and distraught; Jazz, surprisingly, appeared wrapped in piety; and my Ana was weeping. I was standing in the aisle a few rows behind her and watched in silence for as long as I could take it. Then I went and sat down next to her and slipped my arm around her shoulder. I could see that she was embarrassed.

'I was thinking about Mum,' she said, and I knew that this was only partly true.

A Goan couple was seated across the aisle from us, just behind the sisters. The woman was staring at Jazz with a murderous expression on her face.

'Just look,' she hissed to her husband, 'how shameless they are. Look at how they dress, even in church.' The husband, who had already looked, several times, was putting up an admirable show of insouciance.

'Maybe that's how they dress over there,' he ventured timidly.

'They throw them out of their own churches, which is why they come *here*,' she muttered.

I looked at Ana, who was giggling softly through the tears.

***

Marge was feeling a whole lot better by the time we headed out. The interlude with the Lord had also made her more charitable.

'He wasn't always like this,' she began, and I presumed she was referring to Mr Thatcher. 'We've had some really good times, but after the children left it was almost as if everything just came undone. He began drinking a lot more and chasing after hussies.'

'He even made a pass at *me* once,' Jazz voiced in support.

'That's when I knew I had to get out of it. I was losing my sanity.'

'I'm sure you'll find someone else, Marge… maybe right here in Goa,' I said. In the mirror I could see Ana glaring at me. It's tragic when one's every intention is questioned.

'So where do we go *next*?' squealed Jazz, clearly ill at ease with the turn the conversation was taking (no doubt Johnny making his massive presence felt).

'We can head to Dona Paula. There's a new casino there,' said Uncle Joe.

Ana didn't seem too keen, but both sisters appeared excited. In those days there were hardly any casinos in the country, and I had never been to one.

We drove to Dona Paula and it was a pleasant trip, even in Joe's rattletrap. The roads were better and the route was pretty scenic. All through the journey Marge and Jazz regaled us with tales of their past visits to casinos in London and other European capitals. In all these stories they were in the company of wealthy and distinguished gents. I could just about picture Jazz doing this, but *Marge*? Perhaps rich folks in Britain were not that discerning, I concluded.

We reached Dona Paula and climbed a narrow, winding road to get to the casino, which, when we reached there, didn't seem like much, even to me. My only point of reference was what I'd seen in Bond movies, and, I confess, I was neither shaken nor stirred.

A couple of slot machines were placed near the entrance, and inside there were a few roulette and blackjack tables scattered around. In one corner there was some kind of racing contraption, with toy horses and riders doing laps of a miniature course.

It was late in the afternoon and there weren't many gamblers around. The sisters had informed us that free drinks were served in casinos in Europe, whereas here they didn't even offer us water.

We went through the ritual of buying tokens and Ana and I moved to the slots, which turned out to be no fun at all. To me they seemed like contraptions that were designed to steal money. What was regurgitated was miniscule compared to what went in. Ana, too, tired of this quickly and we walked over to a roulette table, where Jazz, at least, appeared to be cleaning up.

Marge seemed more keen on chatting, and after a while she slid her tokens over to her sister and strolled away, with Ana in tow.

This left me alone with Jazz, which was just fine with both of us. I perched on the stool next to her and we sat close together, thighs touching. This was clearly a babe who knew the game (actually *both* games she was playing). She bet on combinations that I tried hard to decipher, and always seemed to win more than she had wagered. When the ball spun around, she placed her hand on my leg and lightly stroked the inside of my thigh, I guess for luck.

There's something about women and gambling, I noted. Every time she won, which was often, she would slide her fingers closer to my package. If it wasn't for this, I would've bailed out. Roulette bored me to death, as did all the other folks at the table. I had expected the Casino Royale, but the action here was worse than a round of housie in an old-age home. I stuck around, though, for obvious reasons.

The flirting was getting more intense, and her fingers had almost reached the spot. I'd already begun stirring in anticipation, when Marge and Ana strolled back in.

She was smooth, I'll give her that. She withdrew her hand in the most casual manner and Ana didn't seem to notice anything. They walked up to us and I could see that Marge had been crying. Ana had her arm around her waist and was holding her tightly. She gave me a wan smile, which made me feel pretty shitty. She was the best thing that had happened to me, and I'd still managed to fuck it up.

'So, are you guys winning?' Marge asked.

'Yep,' answered her sister, her eyes on the ball. I remained silent.

'Are you all ready to leave? We'll miss the cruise otherwise,' said Ana.

'What cruise?' I asked.

'We thought we could all take a cruise on the river, in one of those launches. I was going through the guidebook and it seemed like fun.'

'Okay,' I said, unconvinced.

Jazz wasn't too pleased about cashing in her chips. She'd been on a roll, even in a joint like this, where the odds were so obviously with the house. Marge, however, was having none of it.

'I didn't come to Goa to spend time in a *casino*, Jazz,' she voiced in a petulant tone. 'I can get enough of that at home.'

'All right, *all right*,' said her sister, making a face at me. 'You're getting to be a real bore, Marge. I hope you realise that.'

Marge looked like she'd start blubbering all over again.

'C'mon, Jazz,' I winked at her, 'I'm sure it'll be a lot more fun than hanging around here.'

CHAPTER 14

A few months after moving to Bangalore I slipped into an existence that I'd only dreamed about.

That first dinner led to many others, and Ana started spending a lot of time in my digs. This would've been a task for anyone else, but she managed to charm my crotchety old landlady, which was a feat if ever there was one.

But it was only after we were officially a couple that she began introducing me to her social circle.

Ana's mum, Aarti, was a divorcee, a Syrian Christian from Alleppey who, I gathered, had been rather avant-garde for the time and place. She had left home in her teens, landed up in Bangalore, and had modelled on the side while pursuing a career in fashion journalism. During this period, she met and married Ana's dad, who was the scion of an established business family.

This turned out to be a disaster, as Aarti was too outspoken and bohemian for the conservative Kannadigas. Besides, Ana's grandfather wanted his son to enter politics, and felt that images of his daughter-in-law in fashion mags, cigarette in hand and clad in revealing outfits, did not make for an aspiring politician's wife. One thing led to another, and by the time Ana and I began dating, they had long since separated.

Ana hardly ever spoke to her father, though he still footed all their bills. Her mum lounged around their house in Benson Town, doing damn all, as far as I could see. She had transformed into one of those society matrons who would espouse any and all causes, passionately, but for limited durations. It didn't matter what the cause was, as long as it was liberal, earth-shaking and, most importantly, didn't drag her away from her card games, movie outings and frenetic bouts of socialising.

Ana idolised her, though I failed to see why. Perhaps she had inherited enough of her dad's conservatism to be attracted to what she considered the wild side. I knew that this was what had drawn her to me. Apparently, before yours truly turned up, she'd had only one real boyfriend, an alcoholic who called himself a poet. She had shown me some of the stuff he'd penned, and it was pathetic, though I didn't tell her this till much later. I guess I was a lot more sensitive in those days.

Anyway, her mum and I hit it off from the very beginning. She was kooky and off-centre, and a tad pretentious as well, but she exuded warmth, and welcomed me into their family. This probably didn't count for much, as Ana informed me during one of our spats. She'd been crazy about the poet as well.

But I still lapped up all the affection. Most mothers, I knew, would go to great lengths to steer their daughters *away* from guys like me.

***

On most evenings I would land up at their place after work and then spend my time shooting the breeze with Aarti until her daughter got back home. At the time, Ana was attending an art appreciation course in a nearby college. Before that it had been photojournalism. Both mother and daughter were dabblers, and who could blame them. Given half a choice, I would've been the same. Most folks go to work every morning out of compulsion, and not to change the world.

Aarti was generous with her drinks, and there was always plenty of Scotch around the house, though all she ever drank was dark rum. This I would pick up for her from the army canteen, though she asked me more than once not to. She also insisted that I call her by name, although, in true army fashion, I'd tried giving the whole "ma'am" thingie a whirl.

Almost every evening she would have folks over, older coots (many of whom were in love with her) who babbled on about the Swinging Sixties,

Woodstock and long-dead writers. It was one of these gents who introduced me to Bukowski, for which I will always be grateful.

Ana would show up a while later, and then she and I would go up to her room. That was the great thing about Aarti: she had raised a fabulous daughter all on her own, and she was still woman enough to allow her to become her own person.

This, of course, was convenient as far as we were concerned. We made love almost every day (and sometimes two or three times a day) in Ana's room. She was as needy as I was, and, compared to her sozzled poet, I might have been an improvement.

Aarti insisted on conversing in Malayalam, which was fine with me as, thanks to Ammama, I was quite fluent in the lingo. Ana spoke the language, too, but poorly, which was a source of much amusement and banter.

It was around this time that I began thinking about getting hitched. I was closing in on thirty, and at least chronologically it seemed the right thing to do. Ana was much younger, barely out of her teens, but she claimed that she couldn't imagine a life without me. Aarti, I knew, would give us her blessings in a heartbeat, which only left the pater *in absentia* to deal with.

The problem was that I could never give her the life she was accustomed to. And I would not consider moving in with them, as both mum and daughter had often suggested.

My career in advertising was chugging along reasonably well. Curry, with plenty of support from me, had managed to turn the branch around, which also meant that I was promoted to Creative Supervisor. The only person I supervised was myself, but in the ad world they dish out titles like dung from a buffalo's arse.

There were also persistent rumours that Curry would be transferred to the Bombay office, which he discussed with me on a daily basis. He kept insisting that he would take me with him, thinking that this would please me, but it didn't. I was madly in love with Ana, enjoyed the laid-back pace of Bangalore, and had absolutely no plans of shifting.

When the call finally came, it was I whom they wanted to bring back to Bombay, but I informed Venu that I wasn't budging. At first, he fed me the corporate ladder bullshit, but when he realised I wasn't biting, he relented. And so I continued to stay on in the Garden City.

***

Life plodded along at a slothful Bangalorean pace, and I was reasonably content for a while, but then this, too, began wearing thin.

The problem was that I did not enjoy my work. For me it was only something that paid the bills. I wanted to be a writer, the real thing, not dish out copy for shampoos and sanitary napkins. But after an entire day at the office doing precisely this, I was too exhausted to write anything else.

And then there were Ana's buddies.

In the initial months of our courtship we hardly ever socialised, preferring to spend time at home with Aarti. The folks I met there were pretty decent, a tad pretentious perhaps, but still tolerable.

The younger lot, to whom I was introduced later, were, to put it mildly, insufferable.

What happened was, like with most couples, our conversations had begun petering out. The lovemaking was still intense, and plentiful, but somewhere along the way Ana figured that our relationship could be livened up by sending in the clowns.

Well, it worked for a while, and then it didn't.

There was a phase in our relationship when we were going out to pubs and discos almost two or three times a week, and this was when the social divide became apparent. Tariffs were high, which meant that Ana was the one footing the bills, and all I could contribute was comic relief.

On one of these nights out, we were in a lounge bar with a few of Ana's buddies, chugging beer and listening to some great stuff from the seventies and eighties. It started out as a pleasant enough evening, and the music was just loud enough to discourage conversation. The last thing I needed was to hear about foreign trips or expensive acquisitions.

This was when our hero strode in. He was an ex-flame of Ana's, one of those pretty boys who'd filled in the gap between the poet and me, and he had swung by to check out what he'd been traded in for, or so it seemed. Initially, Ana was on tenterhooks, but when she saw that I wasn't bothered, she appeared to relax. For all my other shortcomings, jealousy just isn't my thing.

He was funny, I'll give him that, and wealthy *and* great-looking. I found myself wondering why Ana had dumped him, and I'm sure there were others at the table who were thinking the same thing.

In the beginning he was pleasant to everyone, *moi* included, but then I think the burden of being charming and humorous and gorgeous all at once began getting to him. Besides, Ana was cuddled up against me, and I could see that this was bothering him.

After a while, when enough drinks had been consumed, and the follies of familiarity had set in, he honed in on me.

'So, what is it that you do?' he asked, loud enough for everyone to hear.

I work in advertising,' I said.

'Ana tells me you were in the army.'

I didn't say anything. It was all very raw then, and I didn't want to talk about it.

'Well?' he said, after a while. I could see that the kids around the table were looking at him expectantly. Ana had told me he was a very funny guy, always the life of the party.

Wrong night, though, I was thinking, wrong party.

'Well what?' I asked.

'Were you in the army?'

'Yeah… for a bit.'

'Saw any action?'

'Yeah.'

'Where?'

'I don't want to talk about it.'

'Oh, what have we here… a *modest* soldier,' he laughed; '*that's* a rarity.'

I knew what he was trying to do. He wanted me to react, so that I'd look like a boor in front of Ana and her friends… trash from the boondocks, who didn't deserve to be there.

I should've sat there quietly and taken it. God knows, I'd taken a whole lot worse in the army. But I hadn't learnt then and I didn't want to start now, not with this dick.

I gave him a broad smile, drawing him in.

'So, when did you and Ananya hook up?' he asked.

'Sometime after she dumped you, I guess,' I replied evenly.

There were a few suppressed snickers, followed by a long pause. Billy Joel crooned *Uptown Girl* in the background (quite aptly, I thought).

'That's not how I remember it,' he said, looking around. Our group was silent. He was a star in their midst, and one didn't speak to him in that manner.

'You want to tell us what happened?' I said.

The fool was staring daggers at me, but said nothing.

'She told *me* that she couldn't be with someone who was so unsure of his sexual orientation.'

It was a low blow, mostly because it was true. Ana had told me once that she suspected he was bisexual. It was painful, embarrassing, and extremely unfair to her, but I was past caring.

There was a collective gasp around the table and I saw his face coil into a snarl. The gloves were definitely off.

'Listen, you fucker,' he began, jabbing me in the chest with his forefinger. We were both standing now, and he was tall and wide and appeared to be in great shape, but he didn't know the first thing about brawling. You never expose a weak part of your body to an opponent, especially not a finger. There's just too much leverage.

I let him poke me a few times and then I grabbed hold of his pointer and twisted. All at once our hero was on his knees, squawking.

'Vic, *nooo*,' Ana screamed, but the bloodlust had already set in.

'Get up,' I said, yanking on his finger, and obediently he rose to his feet.

I walked him a few paces and then put a boot in his arse. And they were good boots, too, solid army issue. Our erstwhile hero lay sprawled out on the ground and it was show over.

'Get the fuck out,' I told him.

'You'll pay for this,' he screamed, as he rushed out of the room, but he was blubbering as he said it. The group at our table was very quiet, which was okay, since I wasn't really expecting applause.

We sat in almost complete silence for a while, until Ana, abruptly, rose to leave. I followed her out. The vileness had receded, Ana was weeping and I felt pretty lousy. I'd been out of line and I should have just apologised and been done with it. Not surprisingly, though, I didn't.

'Why are you upset?' I asked, with a straight face.

'You're a bastard, Vic.'

'Really? So, it was all my fault?'

There was a long pause.

'Vic, I saw a side to you that I didn't like at all. There was no need to say that to him.'

'Ana, I don't know if you noticed, at least you didn't say a word at the time, but he was making digs at me all through the evening.'

'He didn't *mean* anything, Vic,' she said; 'that's just the way he is.'

'Well, in that case *this* is the way that *I* am. If you bring two of your boyfriends together for a laugh, then you better realise that things could turn sour.'

'Vic, I didn't *know* he was going to be there. I didn't even know he had been invited.'

'You shouldn't have acted so thrilled to see him, then. Maybe he would have left sooner.'

And it went on and on and on. We didn't speak to each other for an entire week, until finally she relented and called me.

It was a pattern that was to become all too familiar.

Things would be cruising along and then some minor incident would occur (minor, perhaps, by my standards) and the whole thing would blow up, and we wouldn't speak for weeks together.

She said I was callous, which was probably true, and a control freak, which I was not. All I wanted control over was my own frame of mind. What she didn't know was that the slide had already set in, and

I *needed* my rules, my pride and delusions just to keep me from falling apart.

Still, all in all it was a glorious time, and I was genuinely sad when it ended.

CHAPTER 15

I was detained at the cop station for almost a week and then they let me go. By then the matter had been sorted out, payments extracted and the guilty pardoned, all outside the ambit of the courts.

The inspector hadn't specifically asked me to, but I went back a couple of times to meet him. He worked gruelling hours, twelve to fourteen at a stretch, but he always seemed genuinely pleased to see me.

Inspector Kadam was an astute guy, and a decent one, and I often wondered how he coped in the department. His colleagues, for the most part, were cunning, narrow-minded louts, who would in all probability be breaking the law if they were not tasked with enforcing it.

We spoke at length, about the situation at home, my studies and plans for the future. Once again, he suggested a career in the military.

'What you need is discipline, Victor, and you will find it there,' he told me.

I know now that what I needed was a lot more than discipline, but at the time I was so confused that I would grab at anything a man like this could offer.

I guess what I was really searching for was a surrogate father.

Years later, I read that he had sucked on the barrel of his service revolver, before pulling the trigger. The news report mentioned that he'd been drinking heavily.

Discipline hadn't saved him either.

But in those days, he was the only one to offer me guidance, and for the very first time I found myself fixated on a goal.

I began waking up early and going for long runs, followed by a vigorous regimen of stretches, push-ups, chin-ups and crunches.

The National Defence Academy, or NDA as it is more commonly known, is located on the outskirts of Pune city and is considered to be one of the best military colleges in the world.

You join the NDA after getting through a highly competitive entrance exam, followed by a gruelling interview.

I studied hard, harder than I'd ever done before, and for the last three months I confined myself to the house the whole time. I had no friends to speak of and had already distanced myself from the crowd I used to hang out with. They didn't bother to get in touch, either. Inspector Kadam had sent word to Ganesh, and dim as he was, he got the message. In those days, you messed around with Bombay cops at your peril.

I placed well in the exam and was instructed to appear before the Services Selection Board for a personal interview.

A few weeks after this, my dad and I showed up at the NDA campus in Khadakwasla. I'd tried convincing him that his presence wasn't required, that I could manage well enough on my own, but he was adamant on coming.

A strange thing had happened since the episode at the cop station. My dad had found God, or at least one version of Him. He'd given up drinking completely and had begun attending an evening service at the local chapel. As with everything else, this, too, was short-lived, but around the time of the interview he was on the wagon, which was why I let him accompany me.

We took a bus to Pune and another one to the NDA campus, where we bade goodbye to each other. He broke down in tears and kept repeating that I'd be a General some day. It was embarrassing, to say the least, as he was speaking at the top of his voice and the sentries at the gate were smirking.

***

What followed was an intense affair spread over five days, during which a number of interactions were scheduled which supposedly delved into every aspect of one's psyche.

I aced the physicals, and thought I performed quite adequately in the interviews. The psychological profiling, though, was what almost got me rejected.

I learnt about it only later, from a batchmate who was posted at the Military Secretary's Branch in New Delhi. This is where every record of an officer's career is meticulously preserved, from the time he appears for the SSB. It can be accessed when a candidate comes up for promotion, or, as in my case, a disciplinary hearing.

The applicant has an aversion to all forms of authority, it stated, probably arising from a deep-rooted sense of insecurity. Also possesses an innate tendency towards violence.

I still don't know why they selected me. Maybe I was a test case, or maybe they thought their system could hold me in check.

And I guess it did, at least for a while.

***

The first thing that struck me about the other cadets was how skinny they all were. There didn't appear to be a spare ounce of flab in the entire academy.

Life in Bombay had been easier and I was bigger than most of them. I stood over six feet tall in my socks and weighed seventy kilos. Not large by normal standards, but out there I was considered a fatty.

Many of the recruits were from military or Sainik schools spread across the country. They were fit, disciplined and incredibly driven. Coming from a civilian background (and that, too, being raised in Chez Gabriel) my levels of discipline and training were nowhere near these automatons. Also, from the beginning, I displayed the aforementioned distaste for authority.

Each new recruit is assigned to a unit called a squadron. In the NDA, squadrons or squads are named Alpha, Beta and so on, and each one has its own building, in which are contained the dorms, offices and common areas. I was consigned to K Squadron, Kilo Squad, or the Killers, as we called ourselves. I'm not sure whether it was by design, but the hardest nuts in the Academy seemed to have landed up there.

There is a special kinship that prevails within each squad, coupled with a casual brutality that is deemed necessary to instil the right measure of toughness in an aspiring officer.

Unfortunately for me, owing to my height and weight (and general demeanour, I guess), I was singled out by some of the seniors for special attention. Unfortunately for them, I, not having been through the grind of a Sainik school, felt quite strongly about this.

A few days after I had moved in, they set upon me in the common room, where a group of us first-years was watching a match on television.

All of us stood up, as we were required to do in the presence of seniors. We were then instructed to move to the back of the room.

There was a ferrety looking bastard called Bittu Yadav, who was rumoured to be close to our squad leader, Randhawa. This guy, I found out later, had clocked me on day one and marked me out for special treatment. Probably figured that his standing in K Squad would go up if he came down hard on the big fella.

Ah, the follies of human nature.

They lined us up against a wall and began shooting questions at us, machine-gun style. Initially, it seemed like fun and games, but then they started getting rougher.

Yadav had positioned himself in front of me, with a lackey on either side. All of them were glaring at me.

'Where are you from?'

'Bombay,' I replied.

I felt the slap before I saw his hand move. The guy was fast, I can tell you. A year after this, I walloped his arse in a boxing ring, but he was pretty quick then, too, as I recall.

'Bombay what?' he asked.

'Bombay, sir,' I replied. This was the required etiquette when addressing seniors.

He wasn't satisfied, though. Maybe it was because I wasn't afraid. Or maybe it was my sneer.

'Bombay, huh? So you think you're a Bollywood hero?' It was a poor line, even from a punk like him.

'No.'

His hand came up again, but this time I was ready for it. I blocked the blow, held on to his index finger and twisted. With my right hand I grabbed his shirt and pulled him forward, thus preventing the other two from getting clear shots at me. I stood nearly a head taller and began systematically butting him. The pain in his finger was so intense that he had no option but to take the pounding. He started moaning and I could see from his eyes that it would soon be lights out, which was when I released my grip. He slid to the floor and began snivelling. Surprisingly, his cronies did nothing at all. Both of them were in a state of shock, as were my batchmates. Apparently, rookies didn't do these things.

***

A few days after this incident, I was summoned by the top dog, the much-vaunted Harpreet Singh Randhawa. It was a serious offence and I was prepared for a strong reprisal.

As I entered his room, I half-expected to be waylaid and thrashed by a dozen seniors, but this didn't happen. An extremely well-built youth was seated at a desk in a corner of the room. He was sporting a stylish pair of glasses and appeared to be studying. His long hair hung open and caressed his thighs as he sat hunched over a book.

He was all alone and I was both surprised and relieved.

He turned around briefly and gestured to me to squat on his cot, and I did so warily. Bittu was one thing, but this guy was another breed, I knew. He was the reigning boxing champ of the Academy and had excelled in almost every other sport as well. I was about to get my arse kicked by a legend.

Ten minutes later, he closed his book and stared at me. His eyes were a piercing shade of blue and his visage had a gravitas about it... a General in the making, for sure.

'I was informed that you had a run-in with Yadav,' he said. His voice was surprisingly high-pitched, quite at odds with his appearance.

'Yes, sir.'

'What happened?'

'Why don't you ask him... sir?'

'Because I'm asking *you*. When I ask you something, I want answers, not more of your lip. Do you understand?'

His tone was sharp, though his expression hadn't changed, and suddenly I wasn't as cocky as I'd been before.

'Yes, sir,' I replied, and told him my side of the story.

He listened in silence, and then he spoke.

'How many of them were there?'

'Three, sir.'

There was a long pause.

'Yadav crossed the line this time. In the old days it would have been okay. But now there's a new rule about manhandling, and he broke it. Have you heard about the Satpute case?'

I nodded. It had been in all the papers. Rajesh Satpute was a first-sem cadet who had jumped into the lake on the grounds and drowned after a particularly violent bout of ragging. Applications to the Academy had come down by a third, which was probably how I managed to get in. Thank you, Rajesh; may your soul rest in peace.

'Well, we don't want that sort of thing happening again, do we?' he asked.

'It won't happen with me, sir,' I replied, and watched his expression changing.

'But I'll tell you what else we *don't* want. We don't want pups like you thinking they can hit seniors and get away with it.'

I remained silent.

'You will trek to Sinhagad every Sunday for the next four weeks, and you will be confined to the squadron the rest of the time. Is that clear?'

I groaned inwardly. Sinhagad was one of Shivaji's forts in the vicinity and it was a six-hour trek to get there and back. Still, I knew I'd been let off lightly.

'Yes, sir,' I replied.

'Dismissed,' he yelped, and went back to his studying.

***

Overall, my days in the NDA were chequered, not unlike my subsequent army career. I excelled at sports, got by at studies, and had disciplinary issues all through my stint at the Academy. I can recall very few weekends when I was not doing some form of punishment, which included forced drills, PT and, of course, the dreaded treks to Sinhagad.

But I made it through the course (just about, some would say), and three years later I graduated from the Academy, somewhere near the bottom of my class. The next step was getting through the IMA, the Indian Military Academy at Dehradun, and then, finally, I was in the Indian Army, and an officer to boot.

I would never quite make it as a gentleman, though; just not in my genes, I guess.

CHAPTER 16

We piled into the taxi, only to find that Joe had turned into a sullen prick because he hadn't been invited to join us in the casino. Wordlessly, he handed me the car keys and got into the passenger seat, booze bottle in hand. So much for being our driver.

'How was it, men?' he asked, after a period of self-imposed silence. 'You had fun in there, or what?'

'Not much,' I replied for his benefit; 'it was really small, and not what I was expecting.'

He nodded thoughtfully, and in the mirror, I saw Jazz smirking.

'So, where to now?' he asked.

'Girls,' I turned around, 'any ideas?'

'We already told you, Vic — a cruise on the Mandovi,' Ana said.

'What say, Joe?' I asked, hoping he'd say something discouraging.

'You'll have fun, men, it's really good. And you get booze on board.'

That kind of settled it, and we drove to the boat jetty near the bridge. We had over an hour to kill, and so we headed over to a coffee shop for a snack. This time around, I insisted that he join us.

The ladies sat together and I plonked down at an adjoining table, facing Joe. Almost straightaway he launched into a gory tale about an English schoolgirl who'd been raped and murdered by local youths only a fortnight ago.

'Just fourteen she was, men,' he informed me. 'As old as my grand-daughter.'

It seemed to be getting nastier, that was for sure. Such incidents were rare in the days when I was stationed here.

'And the cops, don't they do anything?'

He rubbed his thumb and index finger together.

'Most of these boys come from rich families. Lots of pull they have. Everybody knows someone these days.'

Not true, I thought: I didn't know anyone, except perhaps for Ana. And I was pretty sure that that, too, would end after this trip.

At the next table, the hairdressers were complaining about their sister-in-law. Apparently, they were ticked off at the way she treated their mum, who stayed with her.

'The poor thing is stuck in the house, looking after three young kids, while the bitch trots off merrily to work,' said Marge.

'She never even hugs us when we go over,' Jazz chimed in.

'Yep, and I've never seen her hugging our mum even *once*,' Marge went on. Getting hugged was probably a big deal in their family, I thought, and filed it away for future reference.

Ana, as usual, was nodding as if her life depended on it, as if she was deeply invested in all this drivel. I could see that she had forged a special connection with Marge, and even Jazz appeared to be warming to her. Which was odd; for Jazz, I knew, was one selfish babe. But Ana was like that. I hoped she wouldn't forget to hug them, though. That would just ruin everything.

Post the sandwiches and caffeine fix, we headed to the jetty and boarded the launch. To me it seemed more like a largish boat with two levels. The name of the company was painted on the side in large, blocky letters — Mandovi River Cruises. We ascended a narrow staircase to the upper level and plonked down on metal chairs at the back. The seats were lined up, theatre style, facing the prow, where a stage had been erected. Great, I thought, it was dinner *and* a show, except there didn't appear to be any dinner on board.

The only saving grace was a makeshift bar, which unfortunately was still closed.

***

The boat began filling up quickly. There were quite a few families with young children, and many more single males on the prowl. I was wondering if there would be trouble. With Jazz around, anything was possible.

Pretty soon we were underway. The vessel began rocking on the swells, which made me realise just how much I hated water. I half-staggered over to the bar, which, mercifully, was open, and ordered a *feni* shot. The barman asked me whether I wanted a slice of lime in it and I said sure, why not. This I drained in one gulp and then groped my way back to the ladies to find out what they'd be having.

Marge and Jazz came up with a couple of incredibly complex concoctions — soda, cola, juice and slices of fruit, all in precisely defined proportions — and I was thinking whatthefuck, we weren't at the Taj Aguada. We were going down the river in an ancient tub with what appeared to be some seriously crazy folks in it.

Ana, thankfully, asked for a beer. I know she would've skipped drinking altogether if she hadn't felt a need to bond with the sisters. She pressed a few notes into my palm in a matter-of-fact way that I really appreciated.

Joe had scurried off to catch up with an acquaintance, but now I saw him ascending the staircase.

'What're you having?' I asked. He mulled over this question for such a long time that I thought I would have to bop him.

'*Feni*,' he replied, finally.

'Good man,' I said, and put my arm around his shoulder. He thought I was giving him a hug and moved in to make it easier, but all I wanted was for him to accompany me to the bar and help out with the drinks. It sure was my lucky day, I thought: everyone seemed to want a piece of me.

A while later we were back in our chairs, sipping at our drinks and waiting for the show to begin. Joe had already given us a rundown on what to expect. He knew these cruise boats intimately, or so he claimed, having worked on one for several years. Started off as a deckhand and rose all the way up to MC on the nightly show. When his back gave out with all the prancing and dancing, they demoted him to bartender. He didn't quite finish the story, but I could guess how that had turned out. The friend he had bumped into was a clown in the performance. They had once worked together.

The show started up and they stuck to the script, largely. I knew this because Joe was seated right next to me, forecasting every act well before it began. The only thing he got wrong was the Goan folk dance, which they had replaced with a more contemporary jive performance.

It was pretty standard tourist fare (less affluent tourist, that is). The band was a bit off-key and the MC was falling over himself in an attempt to be witty. The clowns were middle-aged and sad-looking, and not a single child laughed. The jiving was pretty decent, but I guess that's the least you can expect in Goa.

The performance ended with the Konkani masala numbers. The MC invited folks to dance, and pretty soon the floor was packed with screaming idiots. Both Jazz and Marge were swaying in their seats, and Ana placed her hand on my arm and squeezed gently. I guessed it was some sort of cue to lead one or both sisters onto the dance floor.

I declined, however. The boat was rocking badly and I could barely stand upright, let alone do a jig. As luck would have it, I didn't need to, as I had Uncle Joe with me.

'Joe, what're you sitting around like a pansy for?' I said to him. 'Why don't you ask the ladies to dance?' It took him a while to comprehend what I was saying, but when it sunk in he looked like he'd won the state lottery.

'C'mon, girls, letsh dansh,' he screamed, and nearly toppled over backwards as he rose to his feet. This was the guy who'd be driving us back to Baga, I was thinking.

Jazz jumped up, followed by a slightly reluctant Marge. Ana gave me a withering look as she rose from her seat, which I countered with my own "What happened? Why are you upset? What have I done *now*?" one.

Turned out it wasn't as bad a deal as one would have thought, as Joe was one hell of a dancer.

He was seventy if he was a day, but he pranced around on the stage like a teenager. Marge and Ana tried to match him step for step, but it was Jazz who was the star of the show. They'd wound up the Konkani songs and moved on to Bollywood numbers, and this was when both sisters, especially Jazz, came good.

Her dancing was so fabulous that a space cleared on the dance floor, and folks huddled around in small groups, staring at her. Since Ana was up front with the revellers, I, too, had an unhampered view of the proceedings.

She was really something, I had to concede; not beautiful in a conventional sense, but simply bursting with sex appeal. Her sarong was hitched up to mid-thigh and she was shaking her hips and bosom with a manic intensity. It was *bhangra* meets belly dancing, and every man there, including old Uncle Joe, reached wood that evening.

The dancing finally wound up when the boat began pitching, signalling that it was time to dock.

Ana and the sisters groped their way back and Ana plonked down in my lap in a proprietary manner. It was unlike her, but after what we'd witnessed, she wasn't taking any chances.

'You girls were *incredible*,' I said, and they smiled and thanked me, Marge in particular. She was lapping up compliments like a thirsty kitten, and I felt a bit sorry for her.

'How come you didn't join in?' Jazz purred.

I smiled enigmatically.

'I'm a writer, and writers seldom partake... they merely observe.'

'Oh, really...?' she smirked.

'He does dance, actually,' Ana put in. 'And in fact, he's very good.' And it was mostly true. It's one of the things you pick up in the army: the useless stuff, like using a knife and fork.

***

We staggered off the launch and waited around on the dock for Joe. This took a while, as that gent had hooked up with some other cats he'd worked with before.

'You had fun, or what?' he asked, when he finally deigned to join us. All of us replied in the affirmative and the old coot seemed mighty pleased. He wasn't such a bad guy after all, I thought, if you

145

could get past the whining and the stench of stale liquor.

'Where do you want to go now? There are some great parties happening in Margao,' he said hopefully. Our boy was all pepped up and raring to go.

I would've given him a thumbs-up, but Ana put her foot down. The trip had been fun, but I guess not what she'd intended. There was still that small matter of a heart-to-heart, which lay between us.

'It's been a long day, Uncle. I think all of us would just like to head back to Baga.'

I thought the sisters might object, but Marge at least was with Ana on this one.

'Let's go back, Joe. It's been a fantastic day, but we're all a bit worn out,' she said.

Jazz didn't seem worn out at all. She gave me a look, but didn't say anything, and so we all trooped back to the car.

***

'What about dinner?' queried Joe, after we had crossed the Mandovi.

'Any nice places around here?' I asked, before Ana could speak up.

'There's a joint in Candolim. Tasty food, and there's a show, also,' Joe replied.

A show in Goa was a bit of a crapshoot, as the repertoire could be pretty diverse. But, to me, anything was preferable to heading back to our resort.

'Let's try it,' I said with gusto. There was silence in the backseat.

The show turned out to be a game of housie with a drunken announcer and lots of old folks. His comments were so crass and inappropriate that they were actually quite hilarious. I was the only one laughing, though. The girls had tuned out, in tandem, after a comment about Jazz's attire (or lack thereof). Joe had vanished to the back of the restaurant, where no doubt he was being given his cut for bringing us.

The food was great, though, and served quickly, which was a rarity in Goa. We gulped it down as fast as we could and then headed back to Baga.

***

Captain Jack was smack in the middle of a long swallow when we passed him on the way to our cottage.

His eyes were blurry and his face crumpled as he lifted an arm in greeting. I knew what he was experiencing. It was tough to endure your own company when you were as far gone as he was. He seemed to have forgotten his earlier rudeness and made signs for us to join him. I wouldn't have minded, but sensing that the regiment would revolt, raised my hand in reluctant farewell.

At least the ladies would be pleased, I thought, Ana and Aunty Miranda.

CHAPTER 17

Things began to unravel with Ana after Aarti passed away.

Initially, I considered Aarti a bit weird and often caught myself wondering if all the affection she showered on me was genuine, and whether at some point she would expect a *quid pro quo* (not that I had much of anything to offer).

In time, though, I realised that she expected nothing from me, not even that I continue to be with her daughter. Aarti did what she did because that was the person she was, with a capacity for giving that I've never seen in a person, either before or since.

To say that she took the place of my mother would be to oversimplify things, as that was not how I thought of her. Over a period, though, she became what my mum ought to have been to me: a source of unconditional love. It was just that in Aarti's case she had so much to give, and dispensed of it freely.

Ana, I knew, worshipped her, but there were undercurrents there, as there tends to be between mothers and daughters. I'm sure, though, that that was where she got her kindness from, for after Aarti's demise I got a chance to meet Ana's father.

When Aarti was around, I spent almost all of my free time in their home. I was the son, the son-in-law, the driver, errand boy and co-conspirator in all her varied schemes and ventures. She had a certain aura about her which made me *want* to follow her. She was also able to stoke up enthusiasm and a sense of urgency into any project she put her mind to.

Maybe it stemmed from the fact that she knew she was dying. Ana told me later that Aarti had a malfunctioning valve in her heart, a condition she had had from birth. To me it seemed ironic that a heart so strong could give out so soon.

I met Ana's dad for the first time on the day of the funeral. An elegant service was held at St Patrick's Church, and it seemed as if all of Bangalore had turned up.

He drove up in a Mercedes with his current girlfriend, and strode into the church as if he owned it. He was a fine-looking bloke, I'll give him that, elegant and stylishly attired. But he also had an oily air about him. He came to his ex-wife's funeral as if he was the main draw at a social event, greeting and making small talk with all and sundry. A lot of folks seemed to know him, and treated him with a great deal of deference.

Not Ana, though. She was comporting herself with a great deal of dignity, although I knew she was close to breaking down. Aarti had been the fulcrum of her world.

A number of people spoke about Aarti during the service and by the end of it, Ana, who had tried hard to remain composed, was weeping in my arms. Her dad sat in a pew across the aisle from us and was looking at her with concern, but did not come over once to console her. I couldn't fault him entirely, though. It had been years since the separation, and perhaps this was the relationship they shared with each other.

I was introduced to him after Aarti's coffin was put in the ground.

Ana clung to me as folks came over to offer their condolences, while he stood a little distance away, absorbed in an animated chat with his lady friend. I got the impression that she wanted to leave, whereas he felt compelled to stay longer. Clearly there were lines being drawn.

And erased, perhaps, for a few minutes later they walked over to where we were standing. The lady appeared to be fuming. I tried to disengage myself from Ana, who held on to my arm even more tightly.

'I'm really sorry, Ananya,' he said to her, looking right through me.

'Thanks for coming, dad,' she replied.

She was being sarcastic, but he didn't get it, or at least pretended not to. He appeared nonchalant now, as if he was merely going through the motions. I knew that this was for the benefit of the shrew standing beside him, who Ana ignored completely. In that respect the girlfriend and I were being given the same treatment.

'Please call me soon,' he said, a tad too formally. 'I need to speak to you.'

He shook my hand on leaving, one of those firm grips to let you know who was in charge. He was a tall man, and wore the finest suit I'd ever seen. I felt drab and insignificant in comparison.

'The bastard,' she sobbed in my arms when we were back at her place, 'bringing that bitch to my mother's funeral.'

I comforted her as best as I could. The woman, I knew, had been with him for a while, and I guess had entitlements, too.

***

A week or so after the funeral, Ana informed me that we'd been invited to his place for dinner.

'We don't have to go if you don't want to,' she added.

'Let's go… he is your dad after all,' I replied. I'd always wanted to know how the other side lived.

'He's a difficult man, Vic. He can be quite rude and condescending at times.'

'It's okay, sweetheart, I can handle it,' I said, glad that she hadn't met *my* father.

And so, on a breezy Saturday evening, we drove over to her father's home. It was situated in a tree-lined street, just off MG Road, and was set in over an acre of immaculately landscaped grounds. Aarti's home in comparison resembled an outhouse.

It was also very tastefully done up, in a fusion of ethnic Bangalore meets British Raj. The entire property reeked of style and old, old money, and I felt pretty intimidated.

'Quite a place,' I said, trying to sound nonchalant.

'It was much nicer when we lived here,' she replied.

'You used to stay here?'

'For a few years... until he decided to separate from my mother.'

I said nothing. I would need to tread carefully here, landscaped grounds notwithstanding.

The girlfriend wasn't home, we found out soon after being seated, and I saw Ana visibly relaxing.

'Her mother wasn't feeling well, so she decided to spend a few days with her,' her dad informed by way of explanation.

He was as nattily attired as before and exuded a masculine fragrance. He also seemed genuinely glad that Ana had shown up. She, however, had slunk down in a corner of the huge sofa and appeared to have tuned out.

'So, young man, what will you have?' he asked. He had a bluff, salesman's manner about him which Curry, I knew, would have admired.

'Whisky, sir,' I replied.

'Not rum?' he said, and I smiled. It was supposedly an army thing, this fondness for the dark stuff, but for me it had always been more about economics.

'I'd prefer whisky, sir, if you have it.' The jousting had begun.

'Take your pick,' he replied, leading me over to a massive bar which occupied one corner of the room.

I gazed at a selection of single malts that would rival any duty-free. He was clearly a man who enjoyed his drink.

He was watching me carefully to see what I would choose. I'd met pricks like him before, high-ranking officers mostly, who rated themselves against the perceived shortcomings of others. I knew he wanted me to pick something obvious, like Red Label, for instance, which in his world would qualify me as ignorant, and inferior.

What I ought to have done was ask for something so plebeian that it would be a rap on his knuckles. I know that that was what Aarti would've done. Only this was me we're talking about.

When I saw that stash, it felt like I'd died and gone to liquor heaven. There was also a brand I'd been dying to try, having read about it in a book by Trevanian.

'Do you have Laphroaig?' I said.

His face was deadpan.

'Of course, I do. How would you like it?'

'With soda and lots of ice, please,' I replied, and saw his lips quivering. When he fixed his own drink, he poured in just a dash of cold water, about equal to the quantity of whisky in the glass. He looked at me pointedly as he did this, and the message was clear. He was the better man, by far, and I was the boor who was dating his daughter.

I understood at a visceral level why Ana felt the way she did, and why Aarti had only consumed Old Monk Rum.

***

We were seated in one corner of the living area, nursing our drinks and making small talk (or at least two of us were).

Her dad was conversing with me, supposedly, but every once in a while, his eyes would dart towards Ana, who was glancing through a fashion magazine. I was bored, too, but went through the motions stoically. Besides, it was damn fine whisky, rich and peaty, and unlike anything I'd had before.

He was bragging about his various businesses, the folks he knew and his burgeoning association with the state JP, a party he stated was the future — modern, progressive, industry-friendly.

'What's your take on the masjid controversy?' I asked, just to wind him up a bit.

He paused for a moment and then glanced at Ana, who was finally paying attention to what he was saying.

'It was unfortunate, but also necessary.'

'Why?' Ana and I asked in unison. I was a lot less agitated than she was.

'It's a matter of faith. These people need to realise that when they live in *our* country, they have to abide by our rules. They cannot trample all over us.'

And that set Ana off. She went into a rant about the JP: fundamentalism, right-wing nationalism and lots of other things. She wasn't very convincing, or even coherent, but I loved her all the same for it.

To me, the mansion, the booze and his impressive list of achievements meant nothing any longer. Prejudices, more than anything else, reveal what one truly is.

He continued to wear a smug expression, but it was fraying at the edges. I could see that he really cared for her, and that this was not how he'd wanted the evening to play out.

'She's like her mother,' he said to me, by way of explanation; 'she thinks with her heart, not with her head.'

'Don't bring my mother into this,' Ana screamed. 'What do you even *know* of my mother?'

He paused before replying.

'I know that she was irresponsible, wild and carefree. All fine qualities when one is young, but you do need to grow up some time.'

I could see his point, but he didn't know the half of it. How could Aarti have ever got hitched to a guy like *this*?

'So, this is what it always comes down to, doesn't it?' Ana screamed. 'You think that because you inherited this house, and have all these cars and servants, you're better than us.' This, I thought, was a tad unfair. After all, he paid for the car and servants in their house as well.

Her old man had slumped down in his seat. His single malt had turned to tap water.

'Ana, it's not that way at all. I want so much for you. I want you to do so much with your life. You're capable of doing so much more,' he whined.

Which, of course, was the wrong thing to say at that point. Ana knew, better than anyone else, that she was merely whiling away time with her courses and causes and short-lived fads. She didn't need to be reminded of this, and especially not by him. I knew exactly how she felt, though in my case there wasn't anybody to give me advice.

And then, since he'd already messed up with his daughter, he began the process of dismantling me, piece by piece.

'So, where did you say you were working, Victor?'

'G&W, sir,' I replied. I don't know why I kept referring to him as "sir". Guess it was an old army thing.

'And you plan on getting married to my daughter?'

I didn't answer for a while. The question had taken me by surprise. I glanced at Ana, but she was looking away studiously. I guess she, too, wished to know the answer to his question.

'Yes,' I said finally.

He stared at me, thoughtfully, like this was a cross-examination in a court of law and I'd just confessed to something damning.

In the army I'd run into a lot of pretentious farts, but no one to compare with this jerk.

'So, what do you do there?' he asked. I'd sat through enough interrogations to know that he already knew the answer.

'I'm a copywriter,' I replied.

He nodded in mock-seriousness. I could see that he was getting a real kick out of it. Perhaps even saw himself on a movie screen doing precisely this, cleverly exposing his daughter's money-grubbing suitor. He was beaming like a torch, the flame of righteousness burning bright within him, while all I wanted was to knock in some teeth.

'So,' he said after a bit, 'how much do they pay you these days? Can't be very much, can it?'

'Daddy!' Ana screamed at him.

But it wasn't enough, not by a long shot. Too bad he wasn't younger and stronger.

'It's not much,' I agreed, 'but it's enough for me.'

'Probably,' he replied. 'The question is, is it enough for both you and my daughter?'

'Vic, I've had enough of this. Let's leave,' Ana said.

'And one more thing,' he went on, not done with me, 'I have some very high-ranking friends in the Indian Army.'

I waited. Ana was about to say something, but then decided not to. I hadn't shared much with her about my time in the army, just the stint at the NDA and the commando training; standard stuff that every *fauji* employs to impress women. I hadn't mentioned a word about the other things.

'One of them told me that you were dishonourably discharged. You want to tell us what happened?'

I said nothing, but I stared at him for a while and saw him starting to quail. He was a step away from being grievously injured, and luckily for both of us, he realised it.

'Vic, I want to leave,' Ana said, and the fire in my brain subsided and only the burn remained.

When I spoke, my voice was calm.

'You, sir, are a fine one to talk,' I said. 'I've been told a lot of things about you, as well.' My choice of words was intentional, and intended to hurt. I wanted him to think that it was Ana who had told me, when actually it had been Aarti, over several boozy evenings filled with rum and recriminations.

'I've heard that you're one of the most corrupt, unscrupulous businessmen in the country,' I went on. This was, of course, an exaggeration, as the country is quite blessed when it comes to unscrupulous businessmen.

'Listen, *boy*, what do you even know about business?' he yelped, and I saw that the earlier smugness had vanished. He darted nervous glances at Ana, probably wondering just how much she knew about his affairs.

'I admit I don't know much. But I do know that bribing politicians to land government contracts is illegal. I also know that supporting divisive, right-wing organisations to further your own business interests is wrong. And for all your big talk, your houses, cars and expensive whiskies, I know that what you really are is a two-bit hustler who would break just about every rule to succeed.

'And let me add that you know nothing about what happened with me in the army... nothing at all. What you heard was the official version, which was convenient to put out, because, unfortunately, even in the forces there are men like you who would sell their own mothers to get ahead.'

Ana was staring at me in silence. There was a look in her eyes that had not been there earlier, when I was draining his whisky collection. Abruptly, she rose from her seat and held out her hand towards me.

'Get out of my house,' he hissed, but it was unnecessary, as we were already heading towards the door.

***

I took the wheel on the way back and she sat in silence beside me. Tears were streaming down her face and I knew I had messed up badly. Regardless of how she felt about him, he was still her father.

'Vic, what was he saying about your army service?' she asked, when we reached her place.

'It's nothing, sweetheart, you don't want to know,' I replied.

'But I need to know, Vic. You *have* to tell me what happened. It's very important to me.'

I looked at her and knew that what she said was true. A line had been crossed and there was no going back. And in any case, I would've had to tell her some time.

I sat her down and began my story. By the end of it I was sobbing, while she held me in her arms and rocked me. And that's how we spent the night, right there on the sofa.

But it didn't end there, as the nightmares had come back to haunt me.

CHAPTER 18

The dreams were unrelenting and I woke up several times, bathed in sweat and breathing hoarsely. Even Ana, who is the soundest sleeper I know, got up once and asked me what the matter was. My sinus, I replied, and rolled over on my side and pretended to sleep.

***

The next day it was pouring. The rain formed an opaque sheet outside our window and beat down on the roof with a thrumming intensity. We stepped out of the cottage and within seconds we were drenched. Initially, it was fun, but after a while I got tired of the forced gaiety.

We came back to the room and had a long shower together. Ana had always been slim, but now she seemed even more slender. Her ribs protruded ominously and her shoulder blades were like knife edges. Her breasts were still full, though, and her bottom nicely rounded. It had been a year since we'd last met, and in the interim, she'd transformed into a woman.

We began soaping each other gently, and her hands moved past my chest, after spending quality time with each nipple. She then sensuously lathered my stomach and butt, allowing her forearm to brush against Junior, who was standing to attention like a parade soldier.

I couldn't take this for much longer and soon we were pounding away furiously against the bathroom door. It went on for a while and I'm sure Aunty Miranda would have evicted us, had she known.

Afterwards, as we were towelling off, I noticed her weeping quietly. This was something she had seldom done in the past and it troubled me. The last thing I wished to do was to cause her even more hurt.

We were lying in bed, and I was mulling over when to broach the subject of stepping out for a drink, when Ana spoke.

'Vic,' she said in an undertone, 'I need to talk to you.'

The look on her face scared me. The old line came to mind — it's not you, it's me... too clichéd to use, but true nonetheless.

'Sure, Ana,' I said, feigning nonchalance. 'What about?'

'About *us*, Vic,' she said, sounding irritated, 'about where we're headed.'

I did not reply.

'I know we've been through this before, but now I really need to know where I stand... where this relationship is going. I can't continue like this any more.'

'Ana, you know there's not much I can offer in terms of security. I could never afford to take care of you in a manner that you deserve.'

I thought it was a good answer, but she slapped me. It was a hard slap and I was glad I hadn't seen it coming, as I might have hurt her in reflex.

'When will you at least be *honest* with me?' she screamed. 'Isn't that the least I deserve?'

I said nothing.

'You *know* me... and yet you talk like this... like I'm some kind of Barbie doll who could never survive in this world without daddy's money. Why do you *keep* pushing me away like this?'

'Pushing you away?' I managed. 'How?' But she was right. I was simply trying to buy time, and both of us knew it.

'Vic, do you know why I asked you to meet me here?'

Sex and booze were my preferred answers, though not the right ones, unfortunately. Once again, I remained silent. It was safer that way: much less chance of being ambushed.

'I've reached a crossroad in my life, Vic. I can't go on like this, not knowing which way we're headed.'

Still I said nothing. *I* knew where this was going, and it terrified me. I think, somewhere in a corner of my pea-sized brain, I figured she would always be there for me, hanging around on the side-lines until I finally came to my senses. That's what I used to think in those days. That's the kind of fool I used to be.

'I know things are hard for you, I know what you've been through, but I can't go on like this either, waiting for you to make up your mind, for things to somehow sort themselves out.'

'Is there someone else?' I asked weakly.

'You still don't get it, do you? It's not about anyone else. It's about you and me. You must understand that things cannot go on this way.'

'What do you want from me, Ana?'

'You *know* what I want, Vic.'

'That's something I cannot do. Not at this point in my life, and perhaps never.'

She nodded her head slowly. All of a sudden, she went very quiet and it scared the crap out of me. I'd expected her to break down, have a crying fit; that I could've handled, but not this.

'Okay, Vic,' she said after a long time, 'that's it then. I guess you've made up your mind.'

I kept my silence. It was a minefield out there and I wasn't venturing in. Outwardly composed, she picked up a book and pretended to read. A clammy stillness enveloped the room, only accentuated by the raindrops pattering down on the roof.

'I'll just step out for a bit,' I mumbled, and scurried out of the room like a rodent. I needed a couple of stiff ones, and badly.

The Braganzas were well into it when I passed them on the way out. Jack gave me a wide grin and raised his hand in greeting. I guessed that the *feni* had done its part in flushing out any residual obnoxiousness. The crone, however, was glaring at both of us in turn, displeasure writ large on her face.

I took a right at the gate, heading in the direction of Calangute, and a short stroll later I settled on a joint which appeared rundown enough to suit my pocket. The place was almost empty, which was fine by me. In my present frame of mind, I couldn't stomach another conversation.

My copy of *Factotum* was in my jeans pocket and I fished it out after my drink was served. It was lumpy and moist from the downpour, but still readable.

Bukowski is a midday read, when one has just commenced drinking. At night his compulsive need to self-destruct can get to you, but in the daytime he's just glorious, especially in a place like this.

Some day, I hoped to write like him, but it took some doing, I knew. You had to screw up pretty badly, almost make a career of it, to come up with stuff like that. And after my talk with Ana, I wasn't so sure if I wanted to.

After a while, I put the book down. Chinaski was guzzling, gambling, brawling and screwing himself to death, but I wasn't so sure anymore that I wanted to end up like him.

I gulped down one for the road and then headed back to the resort.

***

She wasn't in the room when I got back, and suddenly I was afraid. I couldn't spot her suitcase either and for a moment I thought she had just up and left. But when I checked more thoroughly, I found it lying beneath the bed, packed and ready to go.

There was nothing else to do, and so I hung around in the room waiting for her. I knew that it was inevitable, but the thought of her leaving was gnawing a hole in my gut.

It was only then that it hit me how much I loved her.

CHAPTER 19

Bombay was Mumbai when I got back from Bangalore, but other than that nothing had changed. It was the same hellhole it'd always been, large and faceless, and a putrid mess. But it was still the only place in the world I considered home, and I realised just how much I'd missed it only when I returned.

I had decided, finally, to do what I felt I was meant to do, which was to make a stab at penning down The Great Indian Novel.

This was after things had hit rock bottom as far as Ana and I were concerned. After what must've been our umpteenth break-up, we, very rationally, met up at a coffee shop and decided to call it quits. At least for a while, she qualified, until we figured out whether we were meant to be together.

Okay, I'd said, surprised at the lack of feeling inside me. This was, after all, a girl I'd once wanted to marry.

Since I had decided to chuck it all up anyway, I splurged on an air ticket home. I'd said my goodbyes over the phone and asked Ana not to come to the airport, but she was waiting outside Departures when I reached there.

I was really glad to see her. Ashamed and torn up as well, but delighted that she'd shown up.

She had not applied any make-up and appeared pale and gaunt, but still managed to turn every head in the place. Our goodbyes were short as I was late for my flight, having got roaring drunk the night before.

We walked over to a corner and she clung to me for a while, self-consciously, as the lady cop who was stationed there kept staring at us.

'Stay in touch, Vic. And keep writing. I'll miss you.'

'I'll call as soon as things settle down,' I promised, and moved towards the entrance. I looked back once and she was still standing on the kerb, staring at me. She gave me a wan smile, raised her hand and then turned and walked towards the parking lot.

***

I was half-expecting to find someone at the airport, waiting to receive me, but this was just wishful thinking. The only person I'd informed was my father, and he was so sozzled at the time that very little had registered.

I used to call him every once in a while, and I knew that things were bad and getting worse. He slobbered over the phone line, mouthing gibberish that was becoming increasingly hard to comprehend. It was a wonder that our neighbours still summoned him every time I telephoned.

My dad had not turned up, nor had anyone else, and so I walked out of the terminal and hailed an auto.

Our home was even more of a shithole than when I had left. The stench of liquor hit me as I stood outside, waiting for the door to open, while our neighbours in the lane came out and gawked shamelessly.

After what seemed like an eternity, I heard the soft padding of bare feet approaching. Several bolts were released, and the door was thrown open.

He gaped at me for a while, open-mouthed, and I could see that he'd lost most of his teeth. His hair was scanty and lumped together on different parts of his head, and he had not bathed in weeks. If his had not been a face I had grown up with, I probably wouldn't have recognised him.

A few times, on Ana's insistence, I had invited him over to Bangalore, and was always secretly delighted when he begged off, citing one reason or another. Now, when I thought of this, I felt deeply ashamed.

It had been a while since we last saw each other and I was expecting a hug at the very least. But all he did was tap me absent-mindedly on the shoulder. I followed him into the house and stared at the mess. Almost the entire space was occupied by liquor cartons, stacked up unevenly like a late-stage Jenga game. The floor was damp and filthy, the door of the refrigerator was open, and the stench of rot hung heavy in the air.

This was not a home, I thought, it was a tomb in the making.

He lay down on the sofa and stared at me in silence, and I saw only resignation there. Not a hint of warmth, nor bitterness, not even the glitter-eyed mask of eagerness that he habitually donned when he was ashamed.

I knew he was sick, and probably dying, and I felt terrible, knowing that I hadn't been around to do anything about it.

I had planned to spend a few weeks at home, and then move into my own place. I didn't have a job, but I did have some savings which would see me through at least a few months of rent. Nowhere fancy, but at least not a dump like this. Somewhere I could spend a few extra minutes in the crapper without being verbally assailed.

Now I realised that this would not be possible, or I'd have the death of my father on my hands, in addition to everything else.

***

The next morning, I began cleaning the house with a vengeance. It was a difficult job, compounded by the fact that I hadn't done this sort of thing in years. My dad just lolled on the sofa all the while, staring at me like a zombie and not saying a word.

I would've liked to believe that he wanted me there, but I couldn't really tell. I didn't even know how much he comprehended any more. He was pretty gone as far as I could see.

When the place was all tidied up (relatively speaking), I suggested that we go out for dinner. The empty bottles and cartons had been sold to the neighbourhood *raddiwala* and we had just about enough for a meal.

He didn't say anything, which I took as a yes, and we went to a joint near the Sai Baba ashram that we used to go to earlier. In those days it was only on the most special of occasions. My birthday, the night before Ammama left, and every time he managed to get in touch with my mother.

The place hadn't changed much since the old days, but it did have an AC section now, which we avoided. I don't think he would have noticed anyway. I wondered how he had survived the intervening years. He didn't even have any friends that I knew of.

Suddenly, I was overcome by a wave of sadness, which felt almost pleasurable in a perverse kind of way. There was steel in me, I knew, which could have only come from my mother.

I ordered the staple fare, which is the safest thing to do in joints like this — tandoori roti and butter chicken, and *raita* to go along with it. Times had changed and the price of the *raita* alone was as much as a whole meal would have cost when I was younger.

He didn't say anything and neither did I. There had never been much communication between us, but I got the impression that he was pleased I was back. Or perhaps not. I hadn't really figured out his routine. Maybe he preferred being curled up in a corner with only a bottle of *tharra* for company. It wasn't such a bad existence, especially if you weren't overly troubled by ambition. Maybe the last thing he wanted was for his prodigal son to return and rouse him from his stupor.

But he needn't have worried on that score. I wasn't planning to do much rousing, that was for sure.

What I had in mind was to engage in some serious drifting myself.

CHAPTER 20

She came back an hour later, drenched to the skin, and looking absolutely radiant. Her eyes were red and I knew she'd been crying, but the rest of her was as gorgeous as ever.

'Where were you?' I asked.

'Why? Did you miss me?' she smiled, and I did a mental jig in sheer relief.

'I did, actually. I looked all around for you, but couldn't find you.'

'I took a walk on the beach and it was amazing, Vic. Do you know there's a path from the resort which leads right up to the beach? The waves were simply enormous.'

There was a manic beam in her eyes and I wondered if she'd been drinking too.

'Wow, I wish I'd been there,' I lied. 'I'd have loved to see that.'

'Really? Then come with me... it's quite incredible,' she said. I could sense her underlying desperation, and I felt the blues sneaking up on me, as they often did when I wasn't drinking.

Going for a walk on a rain-drenched beach was about the last thing I wanted to do, but what the hell, it shouldn't always be about me.

***

We walked hand in hand, stepping over sand dunes and tufts of grass on the way to the beach.

The rain had abated somewhat and had settled into a steady drizzle. The sky was overcast and had an ominous look to it, grey and depressing.

But the beach, as she had said, was spectacular.

There was a desolate starkness to it, which one doesn't see except during the monsoons. The sand was a muddy brown and squelched under our feet as we walked towards the water.

The waves were massive, wild and intimidating. I thought about stripping down to my briefs and wading in, but then dropped the idea. The truth was that the sea terrified me. Besides, just squatting on the sand and watching the scenery was intoxicating enough.

I understood where Ana's new-found serenity had come from. There was something so awe-inspiring about the place that it made you forget yourself.

We sat on the beach for a very long time with our arms linked. The sadness had drained away and was replaced by a sense of calm, which was just as unsettling if one thought about it, except I didn't.

The rain picked up, and subsided, and then came down like a squall, before petering off completely. And still we sat there, in silence, staring out at the sea.

Finally, eons later, it seemed, she turned to me.

'Shall we head back, Vic? We need to have lunch.' I had forgotten. Ana was mildly diabetic and needed to eat.

There was a shack on the beach where we had fish curry and rice, with lots of *feni* for me. We then made it back to our room without bumping into the Braganzas, thankfully. They were probably out front, tanking up. I wondered whether Ana and I would turn out like them. At that point, though, it wasn't even a possibility. Our relationship was unravelling, as we both knew it would, but I was shocked at how painful it felt, even to me.

We dried off, changed our clothes and crept into bed, and I realised that something else had changed. When I tried initiating sex, she gently fobbed me off. I was more confused than hurt, as it had never happened before.

'No, Vic, not now,' she said; 'maybe later.'

And I knew then that I'd had my last shot and, as with everything else, I'd blown it.

***

We slept on the same bed, but with a pillow placed between us. It was unlikely that there would be any more lovemaking on this trip, not that it mattered too much. I wasn't used to so much sex all at one go, and my body felt kind of worn out. What I missed, though, was the intimacy, which, too, appeared to have run out.

Ana slept as soundly as ever, while I tossed and turned on the mattress. I had always been a light sleeper, but of late even the few hours I clocked were becoming increasingly elusive.

There's something about watching your own life being flushed away that prevents sleep from happening. It was like one of those loos you find in fancy hotels, where the water and crap swirl round and round, and just when you think that nothing is happening, it all gets drained out in one shot.

***

I had a pretty decent run in the army, before it got all fucked up, and the truth was that for once I wasn't entirely to blame either.

The early years were actually quite enjoyable. Being a Mallu (which makes me at least three-quarters Commie), I found all the boot-stomping and yes-sirring to be rather tedious. But three years in the NDA had instilled a modicum of discipline in me. I learnt that a couple of semi-enthusiastic salutes were preferable to PT on Sundays or a trek to Sinhagad. It took a while, but it did sink in eventually. I would never conform completely, but three years of boot camp ought to teach you something.

Another thing I picked up at the Academy was an abiding love for the written word.

It had started out with Kipling's *If*, which was placed on the desk of every cadet. This poem spoke to me from the very first time I read it. It served as a beacon in my otherwise lackadaisical existence, and the truth is that I tried to emulate each of the concepts laid down in the piece. The truth is, also, that I perhaps succeeded in emulating just one:

If you can meet with Triumph and Disaster
And treat those two impostors just the same.

Not that there were many triumphs to speak of.

The NDA has one of the best libraries in the country, and I spent long hours there poring through reams of the finest works of English literature.

This was when I first thought about becoming a writer. I was into poetry at the time and pretty good at it, too, even if I do say so myself. Not that any of it saw the light of day, as I was too scared of rejection to even consider sending these out to magazines.

Later, though, I began penning down short stories, a few of which were published.

After graduating from the NDA I, like most of the other cadets, enrolled in the Indian Military Academy in Dehradun.

Cadets passing out of the NDA are required to put in a year at the IMA, as compared to direct recruits who are in for an eighteen-month stint. The experience was gruelling, but educative too, even for those of us who had already been through the grind of the NDA.

After a year of this, I graduated as a second lieutenant.

I was never into the pomp and show and forced camaraderie that prevails in the armed forces, and even at that early stage I often found myself wondering what I was doing there. Also, philosophically I was a pacifist, though in terms of temperament I was anything but, and this dichotomy still prevails.

My first posting was in Goa, which was considered to be an easy one. Fast-track career enhancement required that you opt for hardship postings, like the North-East or the Kashmir Valley. Since I wasn't into all that bullshit, Goa was the perfect place for me. Unfortunately, though, it didn't last very long.

For the most part, army life was and still is a sheltered existence, almost completely removed from what most folks would term reality. Physically, life is arduous, but overall, it's like a stint in college. In most cases the friendships made are genuine, your colleagues are men of integrity, and there is a sense of honour, duty and discipline that I have seldom witnessed in the outside world.

What I couldn't stomach was the ingrained servility, the constant bowing and scraping in front of senior officers who I at least could never consider my superiors.

During peacetime, the life of an officer in the Indian Army is quite ordered. You're expected to be up for drills at six, regardless of how much you've imbibed the night before. You are then put through a regimen of jogging, push-ups, chin-ups and crunches for an hour or so. This is followed by breakfast, after which your workday starts. For a junior officer, the job in a peaceful outpost would involve supervising your men while they dug ditches, laid roads and patrolled the countryside. There were also numerous meetings with other officers, non-coms and the local populace, most of which were unnecessary.

Usually you're done by two in the afternoon and then, at 4pm, it's back on the ground for games, which goes on till around six.

Married officers who have been provided accommodation on the base go back to their wives and children, and presumably an evening bonk or two, depending on the mood at home.

For the unmarried blokes, especially loners like me, this was a time for rumination, long spells of reading and, eventually, heavy bouts of drinking.

Liquor is cheap in the army, which was to be expected considering how little they were paying us. Most *faujis* who drink do so heavily, partly to relieve the boredom. There are others who take to competitive sport, which they then pursue to distraction, even going on to win Olympic medals, like that Rathore fellow.

To me, this was merely substituting one addiction for another. Thank you very much, good sirs, but I'll just stick to the bottle.

I had a wonderful CO during my Goa stint, a hard-drinking Parsi named Sorabjee. He never saw any action, and didn't need to, as far as I was concerned. All his men loved and admired him in equal measure. A consummate leader, with just one weakness, which eventually consumed him. All of us expected that he'd make it to brigadier at least, but he passed away a few years later. Cirrhosis of the liver, I was told.

He gave me high ratings in my ACRs, the Annual Confidential Reports that make or break the career of every officer. Which was probably the only disservice he did me, for at the end of two years they moved me out to what was then the biggest fuck-up in the country — Punjab, at the height of the insurgency.

CHAPTER 21

In Punjab, I was assigned to one of the most decorated regiments in the Indian Army. The Rifles had been raised by the Prince of Wales (not the current one, but his great-great grandfather). We'd been awarded three Paramvir Chakras in battle and one of our COs had risen to Chief of Army Staff. The regiment had a reputation for valour that went back over a hundred years, and a history of participating in almost every major conflict since the First World War.

This was probably why we were chosen to be sent to Punjab after the tumultuous events of eighty-four, coupled with the fact that our brigade commander, a crusty veteran of the Pakistan wars, was in the running for a full generalship.

***

The call for an autonomous Punjab was raised after Independence, and there are sections of the Sikh majority who still hold the view that they were promised a sovereign state in exchange for their support during the freedom struggle.

This theory is unsubstantiated, even dubious, given Mahatma Gandhi's resistance to the formation of Pakistan itself. But it was a belief that gained traction in the aftermath of the British Raj.

After a sizeable portion of the Punjab was ceded to Pakistan, a small minority of the Sikhs in India felt that their identity in the newly-minted republic was in threat, and that it was in their interest to press for an independent homeland. A country for the Sikhs called Khalistan, land of the Khalsas, famed warriors of the tenth guru, Guru Gobind Singh.

This was anathema to Prime Minister Nehru, the Cambridge-educated scion of a political family, who had spent almost a decade in jail during the freedom struggle.

One could fault Nehru for a few things, an overactive libido among them, but he was, and remained, a man of principle. He truly believed in an idea of a united, secular India, with no distinctions made on the basis of creed or religion. He had overseen the violent partition of the subcontinent, and was damned if he would give in to one more demand for the formation of another nation carved out of India.

In those days, states were created largely on linguistic lines. When leaders of the Shiromani Akali Dal, the dominant party of the Sikhs, realised that their demand for a separate homeland would find little traction in Delhi, they hit upon the idea of asking for a separate state for Punjabi-speaking people. Punjabi, written in the Gurmukhi script, was also the language of the *Guru Granth Sahib*, the holiest of the Sikh religious scriptures.

A census was conducted and the Hindus in Punjab, who comprised a sizeable number, fearing the creation of a Sikh state, took the position that their spoken language was Hindi, and not Punjabi. This enraged Sikh leaders and led to a fissure in Hindu-Sikh relations, which was to script the trail of bloodshed to follow.

There were other issues as well — diversion of the waters of the Beas to the neighbouring states of Haryana and Rajasthan; the demand for Chandigarh to be ceded to Punjab as its state capital; and the call for Amritsar to be declared a holy city. But all these were minor in comparison to the most pressing issue, the creation of an autonomous homeland for the Sikhs.

What followed was sheer lunacy as far as the Indian political establishment was concerned.

The mandate to govern Punjab was exchanged every five years or so between the Congress party and the Shiromani Akali Dal. The Akalis, though largely peaceful, tacitly espoused the call for a distinct nationhood, and, perhaps owing to this, were able to make deep inroads into the hearts and minds of the populace, especially the rural peasantry. That they did little to press this demand once they had regained power was another matter.

The leaders within the Congress then did what in later years they would accuse our westerly neighbour of doing — breeding a tiger in one's backyard to threaten an enemy, and then getting one's own balls chomped off.

Within the Congress there was an ongoing tussle between the incumbent Chief Minister, Darbara Singh, and the Home Minister of the country, Giani Zail Singh, confidante and key aide to the PM, Indira Gandhi, and her younger son Sanjay.

In a bid to consolidate his position on his home turf and undermine the religious appeal of the rival Akali Dal, Zail Singh covertly put into action a plan to prop up an obscure preacher of the Damdami Taksal by the name of Jarnail Singh Bhindranwale.

Bhindranwale preached a form of Sikhism which was far more extreme in its outlook than that espoused by the largely moderate Akali Dal and its sister organisation, the SGPC. The SGPC or the Shiromani Gurdwara Parbandhak Committee, which controlled all the *gurudwaras* in the state, served as an important source of both funds and political support for the Akalis.

Though fluent only in Punjabi, Bhindranwale, who was universally referred to as *Sant*, or saint, was an immensely charismatic orator. He was tall and whipcord lean, and his gaze was as piercing as the silver arrow that he often brandished.

Initially, Bhindranwale was thought to be a stooge of the Congress, but as his fame grew, he developed closer ties with the Akali Dal, though always holding himself distinct from it. He advocated the path of Khalsa, as laid down by Guru Gobind Singh, and insisted, often forcibly, that followers of Sikhism espouse all the tenets of the religion.

As is usually the case in times of turmoil, folks veered towards the most extreme position.

Bhindranwale had raised a veritable army, funded by crime, coercion and Sikh donors from across the globe, and these men, many of whom were recruited from the ranks of the All India Sikh Students Federation, run by his close associate, Bhai Amrik Singh, unleashed a reign of terror in the state.

Murders, extortion and bank robberies were the order of the day as these misguided youths ran amok. Bhindranwale maintained that he had nothing to do with the mayhem, and that it was a fall-out of the faulty policies of the Congress government; but there were few takers for this position.

He crossed the line when he began actively targeting the Hindus in Punjab. This was when Indira Gandhi, the Iron Lady of India, decided to step in.

By then, the *Sant* had moved into the Golden Temple complex with a gang of followers, armed to the teeth with sophisticated weaponry, including machine guns and rocket launchers.

On 5th June, 1984, Gandhi ordered the army into the shrine to flush out the insurgents in an operation codenamed Blue Star. This would turn out to be one of the most mismanaged combat ops in the history of the Indian Army.

The Golden Temple is open to people of all faiths. In keeping with the tenets of the religion, no one is denied entry and no discrimination is shown to anyone. Visitors to the temple are fed the same simple fare, free of charge, by volunteers, in the *langar* or common dining hall of the *gurudwara*.

Anyone could saunter into almost every structure in the complex, which makes it hard to explain the colossal failure of intelligence in storming the temple citadel.

Bhindranwale and his followers were holed up in an ornate shrine in a corner of the complex called the Akal Takht. From reports that were published later, it appears that the army was clueless about the fortifications that had been erected within the temple compound. These were extensive, well-manned and commanded, and the first few sorties by army commandos were ruthlessly mowed down.

In his so-called defence of the Temple, Bhindranwale had deployed a strategic asset, which should have been known to the army, culled as it was from its own ranks.

A large number of Sikh army officers, some of very senior rank, were sympathetic to Bhindranwale's cause. It is unclear where exactly the disgruntlement stemmed from, but these men willingly chose to throw in their lot with the *Sant*. Chief among them was a former general named Shabeg Singh.

Major General Shabeg Singh was a distinguished officer who had played a role in several Indian offensives against the Pakistani army. His key contribution was crossing over to East Pakistan during the 1971 war and mobilising the resistance movement there called the Mukti Bahini.

He was a decorated war hero, who, towards the fag-end of his career, was embroiled in a controversy, where he was accused of appropriating an army truck through unfair means. With days to go for his retirement, he was cashiered. The General went to court against this order and won a reprieve, but by then it was a case of too little too late.

Disgraced and disenchanted, he rallied to the call of the *Sant* and, using his proven expertise in urban warfare, oversaw the fortifications of the complex.

His skill in this area was apparent from the fact that Bhindranwale's defenders held out for almost three days against a concerted army assault involving elite troops, armoured personnel carriers, tanks and helicopters.

The bodies of Jarnail Singh Bhindranwale and members of his intimate coterie were retrieved by the army from the basement of the Akal Takht. It is believed that they were killed in the artillery barrage from the tanks, which had almost razed the building to the ground.

The outrage amongst the Sikhs was deep and widespread. They viewed the attack on their holiest shrine as a grave and personal insult which needed to be avenged.

Months after the assault, the Indian PM who had ordered the action was brutally martyred. In retribution, Congress party leaders, desperate to make a mark in the changing political landscape, led mobs of angry youths through Sikh localities in Delhi, where they indulged in a shameful orgy of murder, pillaging and rape. Over three thousand Sikhs were believed to have been massacred in this pogrom.

The Sikhs as a community felt completely disenfranchised. First, it was the attack on their holy shrine, and then the genocide in the capital. Post this, and for a decade after, Punjab became a cauldron of violence, power-broking and corruption, which threatened to consume the entire country. Over thirty thousand civilians are believed to have been slaughtered during this period.

It was into this cesspool that the army was sent, with orders to clean up the mess.

CHAPTER 22

In the years following the attack on the Golden Temple, Punjab became the stage for a terrifying free-for-all, with the largely peaceful struggle for an autonomous state being replaced by a casual mayhem that was bereft of a unifying cause.

Gangs of criminals, armed with guns and ammunition from across the border, roamed the countryside, terrorising the citizenry. Extortion and kidnappings were the order of the day, liberally interspersed with bank heists and contract killings. And unlike earlier days, when there was at least an ideological basis for the struggles, it was mostly a case of amassing riches as long as the going was good.

The police in general had become so demoralised by threats from militants that they simply stopped reporting for duty. And, as is often the case in such situations, there were those among them who threw in their lot with the insurgents. All across the state, cop stations had been converted into fortified bunkers, and what went on inside in the name of justice was a travesty.

Human rights organisations were dredging up cases where thousands of Sikhs had been unlawfully detained by the police, tortured in custody, murdered and then cremated in secret. The bodies of many other victims were found floating in canals that criss-crossed the countryside.

Youths were picked up at random, very often their only crime being that they were related in some way to a suspected militant. They were then held in custody for weeks, and bullied and battered in police lock-ups, while their families waited fearfully for any news about their loved ones.

Landowners I interacted with told me that it was easier dealing with the insurgents. They were less greedy, and kept their word, for the most part.

***

We were deployed in January, when the chill was in the ground and winds that blew across the plains could freeze the balls of the hardiest *jawan*.

Our battalion was based in an army camp on the outskirts of Amritsar, and we were entrusted with search operations in the surrounding countryside. The army had established bases all over the state, and road-blocks were set up at periodic intervals to prevent the free movement of militants. We then commenced combing operations, especially at night-time, in a bid to flush them out.

The terrain of the Punjab is mostly flatland and thus ideal from the standpoint of a superior attacking force. There are few hills and forests where insurgents can hide out, and if one has the local populace on one's side, the enemy can eventually be flushed out.

The fields were generally located on the outskirts of villages, but there were houses situated amidst the fields as well, and it was usually these that the brigands targeted. They would enter these residences in the middle of the night, brandishing country-made pistols and AK-47s, and demand to be fed. When they were done eating, they would ask for money and provisions, which the inhabitants were forced to cough up. Reporting these incidents to the cops was an ordeal that was best avoided, for, depending on the mood of the concerned SHO, he would either register a case, grudgingly, or would accuse the farmer of colluding with terrorists and demand a heavy bribe to quash the matter.

By the time we arrived, the law and order machinery in Punjab was in shambles, and the citizenry, bereft of options, began collaborating with the army. We were perceived as redeemers, rather than as an occupying force, and they threw open their hearts and hearths to us in true Punjabi fashion.

We did most of the work, but the Punjab Police was allowed to take the credit. The politicos and *babus* in power wished to create an impression that it was business as usual, a law and order problem that was being handled by the state administration. The truth, though, was very different.

Many of the ops were launched in tandem, with the cops providing us with local intel that proved to be invaluable. They would receive tip-offs from their informants that suspected insurgents were holed up in a particular house. We would then throw a cordon around the entire village to prevent anyone from escaping, following which a joint team comprising army personnel and police sharpshooters would storm the location.

Very few prisoners were taken and even those who opted to surrender were usually bumped off by the cops in staged encounters.

***

It was around this time that I was involved in a skirmish that won me a Sena Medal.

I was a lieutenant at the time and out on a night patrol with my platoon. We had received intel from the local police that insurgents had been spotted in the area.

We were camped in a field adjacent to a *nallah*, and my *havildar*, a callow-faced youth from Andhra called Rao, was squatting beside me. It was close to freezing and he was puffing away on a cigarette, which was against the rules, but what the hell. I had a hipflask on me and was swigging away as well. We weren't expecting any action. We'd been on these patrols several times before and had returned to base with nothing to show but frozen arses.

All at once I sensed movement in the adjoining field. A group of five or six men was heading in our direction. I snatched the cigarette from Rao's mouth and snuffed it out in the mud.

I then gestured to my men to spread out, in case they were armed, not that we were expecting much resistance. The insurgents seldom fired at us and even when they did it was sporadic return fire to distract us before they disappeared into the wheat fields.

We waited until they got closer, and we could spot the rifles slung across their backs, clearly outlined in the moonlight. When they were almost upon us, on my signal, one of the *jawans* let out a piercing yell. They froze in their tracks, and started bunching up against each other instead of diving to the ground. Not an experienced crew, I gathered.

It was then that Rao committed a blunder that would cost him his life. He was only a young lad trying to be a hero, so one couldn't blame him too much.

He stood up, pointed his rifle at them and ordered them to surrender. Now that they knew where we were, they began firing at us. Two of my men were hit by AK-47 bullets, including Rao, who was almost torn in half.

The rest of us returned fire, but they were on the ground now and we couldn't spot them easily. I gestured to my men to lie down in silence. If they moved, we could always open fire, and they had to move, eventually. Daylight was only a few hours away and they needed to be gone before then.

As expected, they lay there for a while and then began moving out. I waited for some time to elapse before shooting a flare into the sky, which turned night into day around us.

They were staring at us like deer caught in the headlights when we mowed them down.

Five terrorists wiped out, one of my men killed and another grievously wounded, and a Sena Medal for me.

Back then it seemed like a very big deal, though now not so much.

CHAPTER 23

In the winter of 1991, my platoon was posted on the outskirts of the village of Tarn Bari. We were encamped in the middle of the fields, where icy winds blew freely, and to make matters worse, there was a virus in the air. I put in a request for an army doc to be sent out and was informed by my prick of a CO that they were understaffed, and (like good soldiers) we had to tough it out.

We had only just set up camp and I had not yet paid a visit to the village headman, as was customary. And so, a few days later, wheezing and coughing, I got into a jeep with my subedar-major, a genial Sikh called Kartar Singh.

The village *sarpanch* was a wiry old man who stood well over six feet tall. He welcomed us warmly, heard me out in silence and then summoned his wife. This lady came and stood at the doorway of their hall. She was tall, too, but in the buxom way of Punjabi women.

'Take care of this boy, *jaan*,' the headman said, 'he's very ill.'

My subedar smiled and said something to her in Punjabi that I did not catch.

She walked up to me and, as is customary in the forces, I rose to my feet. She reached up and placed her palm on my forehead.

'He's burning up,' she pronounced, and then held my arm in a grip that could've dented steel. I tried protesting, but it was pointless. The truth was that I was feeling feverish and drained, and I reasoned that a few hours of rest would do me good before the night patrol.

***

I spent the next four days swaddled in a blanket in their guest bedroom. I hadn't realised it then, but I was running a fever of a hundred and four, coupled with severe bouts of coughing.

They took care of me like I was their own. The lady was at my bedside almost all through the day, sponging my forehead and chest with ice water to bring down the fever, and the old man made me swallow a host of pills and herbal concoctions, which I found difficult to keep down.

I learnt that the headman, Manjeet Singh, in whose house I was laid up, had been a nursing assistant attached to the Sikh Regiment. He ran a clinic in the village and everyone referred to him as Daakter *saab*. He had two sons and a daughter, and, by the manner in which he spoke of her, I deduced that she was his favourite. She was studying to be a doctor in Amritsar, and visited only on weekends.

Their elder son, Ravinder, was, as his dad put it, away. He had left home a few years earlier and the old man claimed that no one knew of his whereabouts. They were hoping that he had fled to Bombay or Delhi, or even *vilayat*. His mother offered prayers at the *gurudwara* every day for his well-being, I was informed.

He was a strong lad, his mother informed me, and had planned to join the *fauj*, the Indian Army, like his father and grandfather before him. But then the attack on the Golden Temple happened and something changed. He was picked up by the cops on a charge of loitering and spent two weeks in jail, before they were able to raise the amount that the SHO was demanding for his release.

When he was finally let out, the signs of the battering were evident on him. His torso was covered in bruises and the muscles on both thighs had been damaged where they applied the roller on him. She had queried him about what had happened inside, but he never said anything. After this, he was not the boy he used to be, she informed me tearfully. Something had hardened inside of him.

A year later he had left their home, she said, and they had never seen him since.

He was not a bad boy, she told me repeatedly. All he had wanted was to join the *fauj* and fight for his country like his father and grandfather.

Their younger son, an amiable fellow by the name of Ranjeet, was still in school, and they were desperate to keep him there until it was time for him to apply to the army. This kid was intelligent, polite and very good-looking, despite the wispy curls that had begun sprouting on his chin. He had an easy charm and a way with the ladies, as was evident from the large number of neighbourhood fillies who would drop in on any pretext.

I think he was a bit in awe of me initially, but after a while he took to spending long hours by my bedside, quizzing me about army life and the selection process to get in.

By the third evening, I insisted on dragging myself to the living room and having a drink with the men.

On the morning of the fifth day, I felt well enough to return to camp. Ranjeet and his father hugged me and made me promise that I would visit frequently. The old lady placed her head on my chest for a moment and kissed me on both cheeks. She told me that I reminded her of her elder son, the one who had gone away.

I hugged her, then bent down and touched her feet, something I had never done before, or since.

CHAPTER 24

What with the Punjab ops gaining momentum, it was a hectic time at our base and, much as I wanted to, I couldn't go back to visit as I had promised. In the meantime, Manjeet Singh had rung up a few times to check on how I was doing.

Finally, after a couple of weeks had lapsed, I requisitioned a vehicle and made the trip to his village. Our jeep pulled up in their compound with Kartar Singh at the wheel, and I jumped out, perhaps a tad more flashily than was required. I wanted to show them that I was as fit as ever, and not the namby-pamby they'd nursed back to health just a few weeks earlier. Kartar followed, hefting a carton of rum that I had picked up from the CSD.

I rang the doorbell and we waited for a while, but there didn't appear to be anyone at home. Disappointed, I was just about to turn and leave when I heard footsteps approaching the door. The bolts were drawn back and we heard the chain being snapped into place.

'Yes?' a female voice queried in English from behind the half-open door. 'What do you want?'

'Is Manjeet Singh*ji* in?' I asked.

Kartar, who was standing behind me, rattled off a few sentences in Punjabi. I heard my name being mentioned, pronounced as Bictor.

The door closed, the chain was dislodged, and then it opened again.

'I'm so sorry, sir. I was having a bath upstairs and I didn't hear the doorbell ring. Please come in.'

To say that I was rendered speechless would have been an understatement. I was tongue-tied, flabbergasted, struck by the proverbial thunderbolt.

'Where are Manjeet Singh*ji* and Aunty*ji*?' I asked, and it came out as a stammer.

I watched as her face clouded over.

'They've been summoned to the SHO's office. I thought at first that you, too, had come in that connection.'

'Why?' I asked.

'We don't know... they didn't say.'

'Where is this police station located?' I turned around and asked Kartar. 'We'll go and check.'

'*No*,' she said. 'Please…'

'Where is Ranjeet?'

'He was summoned as well.'

'But he's only *fifteen*,' I said. What could the police want with a fifteen-year-old?

'They should be back soon,' she said. 'It's happened a few times before.'

I wondered whether we ought to stay. It could be misinterpreted in a small village like this. But I didn't want to leave her all alone, either.

I had seen photographs, which her mother had shown me, of when she was younger. She had pigtails in most of these, and in one she was missing a front tooth. There were no recent pictures of her, which was understandable. Miscreants in the garb of insurgents could march into any one of these houses and demand food, provisions and money. At times they would even molest the womenfolk, we had heard. This was probably why Simar had been sent to Amritsar to complete her studies.

This was also why we were, for the most part, welcomed in the state, even though tales of police brutality and army excesses constantly did the rounds.

'What can I get for you, sir? Would you like tea or *sarbat*?'

'Tea would be great, thanks,' I replied.

She was well aware of the effect she was having on me, and I could see that she enjoyed it. But she was also extremely nervous.

She served us tea and biscuits, after which Kartar informed me that he would wait on the porch outside. This left me alone with her.

We were both silent for a while and then, almost simultaneously, we began speaking, she about her college in Amritsar and I about life in the army. But the tension was palpable, and after a while I couldn't take it any longer.

'I'll go there and find out what's happening,' I said, rising to leave.

'*No*,' she screamed, startling me.

'I'm sorry,' she said, when she was sure that I would not go. 'It will only make matters worse.'

'You said this has happened before. How come? Why are they being detained for no reason?'

She hesitated before speaking.

'Have my parents told you about my brother Ravi?'

I nodded.

'The police suspect that he is a terrorist, an *aatankwadi*. They feel that we know where he is and that we are protecting him. Each time something happens in this district, my parents and brother are summoned by the SHO and threatened. Once, my father was even beaten up very badly.'

She was weeping now, and I moved over to where she was sitting and tried comforting her. I placed my arm around her shoulder as she sobbed against my chest.

And that was how they found us when they walked in.

I straightened up immediately when I saw Manjeet's scowl, but his face relaxed when he recognised me.

Simar rushed over and hugged her mother. Ranjeet gave me a wan smile and went upstairs to his room. I could see that he had been crying.

'What happened, uncl*ji*?' I asked.

The old man paused before replying.

'These are the Dark Ages, *beta*,' he said finally. He used the Hindi term for it, *Kaliyug*, or the time of Kali. A period of downfall, and destruction.

CHAPTER 25

'Sir, there must be something we can do to prevent this.'

My tone was even, and I was forcing myself to keep things civil, but the turd in uniform seated across the desk from me was making things difficult.

'Listen, Gabriel,' he replied, smirking as he said it, 'I've already told you that that's not the way things work around here. We have been sent in to do a specific job, and we cannot interfere in local police matters. Besides, we need the cops on our side, and if we start poking our noses in their business, they will stop co-operating with us. Our GOC had a meeting with their DGP just last week, and the bastard spelt it out clearly — we either played by his rules or not at all. And you know how high up *he's* connected, right?'

I didn't, and personally I didn't give a fuck, either. But my CO did. He was the sort of guy who loved to wallow around in this kind of shit. The way he told it, it was as if he'd been in the room when the conversation took place.

'There's absolutely nothing we can do at this point,' he went on, 'and the last thing we need is some kind of stand-off with the local cops, especially now that the situation has begun turning around. Do I make myself clear?'

In the army, when things are phrased like that, it makes sense to back off. Sense, though, was not something I had much of, not then, and not now.

'Sir, these people are friends of mine and they're being unfairly victimised. They took care of me when I was unwell, and now they're being persecuted. I can't just stand around and watch it happen.'

'Gabriel, you *will* back off, and that's an order,' the runt screamed. You wouldn't believe it, but the way some folks speak in the army could come straight out of a B-grade screenwriter's journal.

I saluted, turned around and left the room. So much for this year's ACR, I thought, Sena Medal notwithstanding.

***

There was one way I could make sure that they were safe, and that was by visiting them often. Of course, it wasn't my only reason for going over.

Simar was easily the most attractive girl I had met until then, and I sensed that there was something brewing between us.

Earlier, she would visit her parents on alternate weekends, but now she began timing her trips to coincide with mine. She had given me the phone number of the ladies' hostel in Amritsar where she resided, and I would give her a heads-up each time I planned to visit. More often than not, she would land up as well, and if her mum suspected anything, she kept it to herself.

One evening, over drinks, I queried Manjeet about what had transpired at the cop station. He was hesitant at first, but after the liquor had kicked in, he opened up. Simar sat by his side all throughout, encouraging him to speak. There was fire in her, I saw, which she had in all probability inherited from her mother.

'It all started after my son Ravinder left home,' he began. 'He was a born leader and had formed a group in the village, boys mostly, all his age and some even older.

'The army action on the Harmandir Sahib had left us shell-shocked. It was an attack on our religion, our way of life, and it could not go unpunished.'

What about the insurgents holed up inside, I asked: gangs of murderers and *badmashes* owing allegiance to Bhindranwale, who had unleashed a reign of terror across the state?

'And who created these terrorists? Who encouraged them? Who built up Bhindranwale into a national figure to combat the Akalis?'

What he said was true. It was a PM and a Home Minister who later became the President. The former paid for it with her life, the latter with his reputation.

'Ravi was a very sensitive boy, deeply religious and patriotic. All he wanted to do was join the Indian Army,' Simar said, and her father nodded.

'I think he made up his mind to leave after the riots in Delhi.' The Delhi pogrom of '84, in which thousands of defenceless Sikhs were hunted down and slaughtered after the assassination of Indira Gandhi.

'He left the house around five years ago and we never saw him again. We prayed that he had fled the country, like so many other Sikh boys, and that one day we, too, would get a call from *vilayat*, informing us that he was safe and happy there. But it was not to be.'

'A few years ago, my father was summoned to the local police station. My mother and I went along with him, but we were threatened by the SI on duty and told to return home,' Simar said.

Manjeet continued, 'They made me wait there for almost the whole day, forced me to squat on the floor outside the lock-up like a common criminal... I, who had done no wrong in my entire life, who had fought for this country in two wars. I tried telling them this, but they spat on my face. When I informed them that I had retired from the Sikh Regiment as a nursing assistant, they mocked me, saying that that was good, as I would be able to treat myself once they were done with me.

'Finally, after several hours, I was summoned inside to meet the SHO, who was a Hindu. He had a very bad reputation, having kicked a Sikh boy to death on an earlier posting, or so they said. He asked me to sit down and ordered a cup of tea for me, which I did not drink. He then informed me that there had been a massacre in Gurdaspur and that Ravi had been involved. I told him that it was not possible, that my son would never do such a thing.

'He was quiet for a while and then he began asking me where Ravi was. I answered, *truthfully*, that we did not know, and that we had neither seen nor heard from him for over a year.'

I glanced at Simar, who was staring at the ground.

'The SHO had a smile on his face. All he said was, "Fine, if that's the way you want it..."

'He pressed a buzzer on his desk and two men walked in. One of them was a Sikh. I knew what was going to happen and I tried appealing to them. I told them repeatedly that I was an ex-*fauji*, but they wouldn't listen. They dragged me away to a cell in a far corner of the police station and then they told me to remove my clothes. I had stripped down to my *kachcha* when one of them kicked me in the groin and said, "I said *all* your clothes, old man. I'm sure you don't have anything we haven't seen before."

'I tried pleading with them. I was crying, but they would not listen. All they kept saying was that I could end the *tamasha* any time I wished by telling them where Ravi could be found, and that they would not let him know it was his own father who had betrayed him. I kept repeating that I did not know, but they didn't believe me. I realised then that they did not *want* to believe me... that they would get far greater satisfaction from what they planned to do to me.'

'How old were you, uncle?' I asked.

'At that time, I was in my late fifties, but age doesn't matter to men like these,' he replied.

It was true. And it happened in the army as well. We were fighting a war, albeit a low-intensity one, and in circumstances like these, barbarism was often deemed a virtue.

'The cell they took me to was large and filthy, and it had a strange odour to it, which I had never smelt before. Only later, when I was taken there a few more times, could I place what it was. It was the stench of terror, faeces, vomit, urine and death all mixed together.'

Simar was weeping now, and trembling with what could've been either rage or fear.

'My knees gave way and I fell to the floor. There was a third man there, a giant, and he picked me up as if I were a baby. I was not in my senses at this time. I have been in the thick of battle, but it was only then that I knew the true meaning of fear.'

'They tied ropes around my ankles and hung me from a hook on the ceiling. Then they began whipping me with a rubber tube. The pain was terrible, and yet *nothing* compared to what came later.'

'My father still has marks on his ankles where the ropes bit into the flesh. Show him, *papaji*.'

The old man bent over, lifted his pyjama bottoms and rolled down the socks which he always wore. There were thick welts on his feet and ankles.

Tears had begun rolling down his cheeks and he was being consoled by his daughter. The injustice of the situation was killing me. These were decent, law-abiding folks, and Manjeet had even fought in the service of the country. And yet they were being made to suffer, for the unproven crimes of an absconding son.

'I kept screaming and pleading with them to believe me. A hundred times I told them that I didn't know where Ravi was, and that if I did, I would personally hand him over, but they kept on taunting me. I could see that they were sadists, that they greatly enjoyed what that monster was doing to me.'

He paused in the telling and asked Simar to pour him a glass of water.

'After this beating, they strapped me to a metal table and began applying the *ghotna* on my legs. Do you know what the *ghotna* is?'

I did. It was a tried and tested method of torture employed by the police, especially in Punjab and other parts of North India.

The detainee was strapped to a table naked and then a heavy roller was pressed down on his legs, back, buttocks and abdomen and rolled back and forth. The pain was excruciating, and if applied unskilfully it could cause permanent damage, including renal failure. The old man could still walk, so I guessed that he'd gotten off lightly.

'How many days did they keep you inside?' I asked.

'Twenty,' he replied. 'Of course, I found out about this only after I was released. In there, there is no day, no night, only periods of more pain and less.'

'And you were tortured like this every day?'

'In the beginning, two or three times a day. Later, it was once a day, and towards the end it stopped completely. I think they realised that I had nothing to tell them. Also, they had brought in a few boys from a neighbouring village and they were working on them.

'I am not proud of this, but I used to *pray* that they would bring in more people for questioning, just so that I would be spared.'

'What happened then?' I asked. 'After twenty days?'

'They let me go,' he said.

'Just like that?'

'Just like that... no charges, no explanations, nothing. I was taken to the SHO's office and made to wait while he signed some papers. He then looked up at me, calmly, as if nothing had happened, and said, "When you talk to Ravinder, inform him that this is what will happen to every member of his family if he causes any more trouble in my area. Next time it will be your younger son, and after that your daughter. You know what will happen if we bring her in, don't you?" I nodded. "Then convey this to your son."

'I tried telling him once again that I did not know where Ravi was, and that our family wanted nothing to do with him, but he just smiled at me.

'"Just tell him, old man; don't play any more games with me. The next time this happens, it will be your entire family."'

'What did you do then?' I asked.

'What could we do? We didn't know where Ravi was hiding.' Once again, I glanced at Simar, who turned away.

'Luckily for us, there has never been a serious incident in this area since then. I have been called to the station once or twice and slapped around a bit, but this is the first time that all of us have been summoned.'

It was crude and medieval, but also brutally efficient.

Earlier, the insurgents had been targeting families of policemen to an extent that there were mass desertions from the force. The cops, fearing retaliation, would simply not show up for work. Once the army was entrenched in the state and the police started regaining control, they began striking back with a vengeance. They went after the families of militants, many of them simple, law-abiding folks. They were incarcerated, tortured and sometimes even killed, and a clear message was sent out.

You touch our people and we will do the same to yours, many times over. Predictably, the attacks on policemen lessened.

Manjeet and his family were merely cannon fodder in a vicious war — collateral damage, which is the term in vogue these days.

CHAPTER 26

It was evening, and the pangs had resurfaced with a vengeance. There was something about our room which depressed me. The walls had that dank, swollen feel of cheap construction after a downpour, and to make matters worse the electricity had gone off. Not that any of this prevented Ana from sleeping soundly beside me.

I got out of bed and ambled over to the main building to inform Jack about the power outage (and perhaps bum a few drinks if I got lucky), only to find that quite a few of the other guests had had the same idea. A largish group had assembled in the lobby and were squabbling with Miranda.

The crone, to her credit, was putting up a spirited defence. She held on to a walking stick and was using it to good effect, simulating a limp that I'd never seen before. Our intrepid sea dog was nowhere in sight, no doubt cowering in the background while his missus held the fort.

I stood around for a while, but lost interest when I saw how one-sided the tussle was. Miranda hobbled about, ranting and cursing like a pirate chieftain, while the real-life captain appeared to have crept into a hole. Her guests, who were for the most part well-mannered folk, tried for a while to register their displeasure, but on seeing that the witch was unrelenting, they drifted away in ones and twos.

I hung around till after they'd left and then grinned at her in a friendly manner. I was hoping she would invite me to share a drink with her, but the look she gave me could have curdled milk. Not much had changed there, that was for sure.

I walked back to our room, let myself in and crept into bed beside Ana.

Once again, I tried reading, but couldn't bring myself to focus. The words wandered around on the page and it was hard to herd them back into coherence. In any case, I was fed up with Bukowski's indifference. What I needed was passion, and Yeats would've done, though Pablo was better. I knew I didn't have it in me to come up with poetry any more. All I could crank out was hackneyed stuff, Mike Hammer meets Hank Chinaski, and on an off-day, too.

The only thing of value I possessed was lost forever, and I realised this now. Twice in my life I had had a chance at something, and both times I'd come up short. And this was what really hurt, almost as much as the grief of the girl who lay curled up beside me.

***

I craved to get out of the room, to head to the nearest dive and immerse myself in *feni* until the pain receded. But at the same time, I didn't want her waking up in the dark and not finding me there. And so, I waited in the gloom (courtesy Miranda's moth-eaten drapes) and took in the shapes and smells around me. I turned my face towards Ana and breathed her in as well.

Her back was facing me and all I could see of her was a mop of curls. A stray beam of sunlight had wormed its way in and I watched a single strand of her highlighted hair glowing like a filament.

I stayed like this for a long time, without moving, until she turned.

She smiled when she saw me staring at her. Her breasts were uncovered, pointing at me, daring me to touch them, but I didn't.

'So, soldier, when do you want to hit the bars?' she said.

I was glad to see that she wasn't crying any more, that she was determined to be cheerful.

'Ready whenever you are, beautiful.'

'Let's do it then,' she smiled. 'Baga will never know what hit her.' It was a corny line, and at another time I would've ribbed her about it, except it sounded kind of right to me. Both of us knew that it was probably our last night together, so we had better make it count.

It wasn't that simple, though. Ana still had to get out of bed and go through her changing routine, but this time around I didn't complain, just soaked it up like a soldier. Or like a civilian, rather. Soldiers can be anal when it comes to tardiness.

CHAPTER 27

Over the course of the next few months I found myself completely smitten with Simar. Earlier, there used to be a constant feeling of heaviness in my chest, and drinking didn't help to allay it either. But ever since I met her, this had subsided.

Not that we spent much time alone, as there was always a chaperone present. This was not Bombay, and things would play out at their own pace. But there were times when she would brush past me, and though the contact was fleeting, I would treasure the sensation for weeks after.

Her family, I'm sure, knew and approved. My being a Mallu didn't matter to them, as long as I didn't look like one, I guess. They kept telling me that I resembled one of them, a Jat Sikh, but without the long hair and beard. They meant it as a compliment, and that was how I took it.

***

One day, Ranjeet, Simar and I decided to walk across to their fields, which lay on the outskirts of the village. It was a warm afternoon and Simar suggested that we draw water from the well. My sleeves were rolled up and I was working the rope and pulley when she came up and stood behind me, her breasts pressed against my back as she held me lightly around the waist. Ranjeet was sitting some distance away, and if he had noticed anything, he wasn't showing it. He was facing away from us and was skipping pebbles across a stream that bordered their property. I kept one eye on him as I turned towards her. The bucket splashed down into the depths, completely forgotten.

Simar slowly disengaged herself from me. She had a coy smile on her face as she moved away, teasing me, daring me to follow.

Both of us said nothing, but the meaning was clear. She knew exactly where this was leading. We moved towards a haystack which lay in between their fields. I continued to watch Ranjeet, but he didn't seem to be either aware or interested.

We reached the haystack and she moved behind it, away from my line of vision. I followed her, but she seemed to have disappeared. It was as corny and predictable as any Yashraj film, though it didn't seem that way to me.

I waited for a while and then made a sudden rush towards my left, and there she stood, crouched over. I slid my hands around her waist and pulled her towards me. She seemed a bit startled, but then began to relax in my arms.

I held her for a while, until she was comfortable, and then my lips dropped down on hers.

She pulled back quickly and, *filmi*-style, slapped me lightly on the cheek.

'Officer*saab*, just what do you think you're doing?' she asked.

'Simar...,' I said, embarrassed, trying to frame a reply.

'You're going to love me and then leave me, aren't you, officer?' she asked in Hindi, and I couldn't make out if she was teasing.

'No, Simar,' I replied, 'I'm not going anywhere. I plan to stay here and get married, to you if you'll have me.'

Her eyes welled up, and it was only then that I realised just how young she was; not much more than a kid, really.

'Are you sure?' she asked. 'You're not just saying that? You really mean it?'

'Yes, Simi,' I said, smiling, 'I'm completely sure, more sure than I've been of anything in my life.'

She collapsed against me and I held her tight. She was a tall girl, and her forehead was pressed against my lips.

'*Simarrr...*' Her mother had appeared at the edge of the field and was calling out to her. Luckily for me, she hadn't spotted us. Simar rushed towards the old lady, away from me.

'Yes, *mumma*?'

'You'll have to help me with lunch. Come quickly. Where is Bictor?'

'I don't know, *mumma*, he must be with Ranjeet.'

I moved away from the haystack and walked towards her brother.

'What are you doing?' I asked, as though I was really interested.

'Nothing,' he replied.

I could see that he was troubled; and so, with some hesitation, I said, 'What's the matter, Ranjeet?'

He looked at me with his limpid eyes, the pupils brown and rimmed with grey. He had his father's eyes, I thought, as did his sister.

'I think she likes you, Bictor*bhai*,' he said.

'Did she tell you that?' I asked.

'No, she never tells me anything, but I know.'

I remained silent, unsure about what to say. I didn't know where this was leading, and in those times, it paid to be cautious.

'And you? Do you like her?' he asked, and the concern in his eyes made me tell him the truth.

'I do, Ranjeet, very much. If your family agrees, I want to marry her.'

'I'm glad,' he said gravely, older than his years. 'I like you, you're a good man.'

I wasn't so sure, but I would take it, even from a fifteen-year-old.

***

Simar must've mentioned something to her mother because, after this, the old lady began treating me differently. She had always addressed me as *beta*, but now this took on another hue altogether. Luckily for me, most of the males in the household, including miscellaneous uncles and nephews, remained oblivious to my altered status in the family. Manjeet, if he knew, said nothing, nor did his son, and life went on as usual.

I wanted to marry her, but it would not be easy, I knew. They were Jat Sikhs, devout and highly conservative; and I, at best, could be described as a lapsed Catholic.

Simar herself didn't seem to be overly religious, though she followed Sikh customs. I often wondered how she would deal with this hurdle when it came up. For a hurdle it would be, of that I was sure. We were smack in the middle of rural India, where change takes a long time coming.

And then there was the hovering presence of the prodigal son, Ravinder, who, in a sense, I was required to hunt down.

From everything I had heard about him, he seemed to be a deeply religious, reticent youth, who had been greatly attached to his family. There was a strong possibility that they were still in touch with him, though this was dangerous, even foolhardy.

***

After that day, Simar and I became much closer. As far as I was concerned, I was totally besotted. I'd been with other women, but it had never felt like this.

With Simar it seldom went beyond holding hands, or the occasional furtive kiss. There were hardly any declarations of love, either from her or from me. But we spent a lot of time out in the fields, chaperoned by Ranjeet with his back towards us, and yet fully aware of what was going on.

It was here that she told me she wanted to leave the state and settle down in a crowded, faceless city, where no one would know her as the sister of a terrorist. I asked whether she wanted to stay in Delhi, and she said no, not after what had transpired in '84.

She had heard that Bangalore was nice, and then there was Bombay.

'How is your hometown?' she asked.

'It's an incredible place,' I replied, 'but difficult. One has to be tough to survive there… a real *badmash*.'

'Like you?' she teased.

'Like you,' I said and kissed her.

CHAPTER 28

I was having a late dinner with some fellow officers in the mess, and we were well into a bottle of Old Monk, when I received the call. It was Simar's mother, and her voice was breaking, her fear palpable even on the other end of the line.

'Is everything okay, aunty*ji*?' I asked.

'*Beta*, can you come over right away?'

'Of course, aunty, but tell me what happened.'

'They have taken uncle, *beta*... and Ranjeet. They came in a van and took them away.'

'Who, aunty?'

'The police, *beta*, the SHO... he came personally. They thrashed my husband in front of our house, and when Ranjeet tried to stop them, they took him away as well. Please, please do something, *beta*; they will kill him otherwise.'

'I'll be right over, aunty. Don't worry, I'll take care of it.'

My brain was boiling over, but I knew I had to subdue the fury, at least for the time being.

I sprinted over to the men's quarters. What I planned to do was not strictly legal, but, hopefully, I could square it up with my seniors later.

I roused three of our heftiest *jawans* and asked Kartar Singh to fetch the jeep. Not one of them said a word, nor questioned a single order. The Indian Army is exemplary in that respect.

I took the wheel and we reached Tarn Bari in less than an hour.

Almost the entire village had gathered outside their house. Manjeet was a highly respected person in their community. He had treated most of them, and their sons and daughters, often for free, and his children had played with theirs. But the fear of the police was so overwhelming that all of them appeared hesitant about what to do next.

I had expected to find the old lady in a state of shock, or crying at the very least, but she sat calmly in the midst of some older folks who were trying, unnecessarily, to console her. There was courage there, I could see, and perhaps this was what her son Ravi had inherited.

Her eyes lit up when she saw me enter, and she got to her feet and embraced me.

'Save them, *beta*. Please save my son,' she said quietly.

She told me where they'd been taken. We had to move very quickly, she added, as the police had a practice of shifting detainees from one lock-up to another, before "disappearing" them.

I wanted many more of the villagers to accompany me, but the terror was great in those days. In the end, another jeep followed ours, with four or five of the older folks in the village.

***

The police station was situated a few kilometres away. It was a large building with a façade of exposed brick and appeared quite imposing. They had told me that at times the screaming of the detainees could be heard on the street outside. This time, though, there was only silence.

The building had been converted into a fortified bunker. The gate was high and there were sandbags piled up on both sides of it, through which rifle barrels greeted us.

'What do you want?' a man called out.

'I want to meet the SSP *saab*,' I said, projecting a confidence that I did not feel. The anger, though, was real, and it propped me up considerably.

'*Saab* is not here. He left a little while ago.' His manner was respectful, even placating, which had no doubt to do with the vehicle we had arrived in.

'I want to see the SHO then, immediately.'

'What is it regarding, sir?'

'Are you going to open this gate, or should we break it down?'

'Sir, please wait, sir,' he said nervously. 'I'll just go and check with the SHO.'

Several minutes later, the gate swung open and we drove through.

I parked the jeep under the porch. Luckily for us, the place seemed deserted. As we entered, I noticed a couple of cops napping, with their feet up on a wooden bench.

The sentry at the gate had rushed past us into an office, and we followed him inside.

It was a strange scene that we witnessed. There were two young Sikhs, boys really, who were squatting in their underpants holding their ears. They looked up as we entered and I could see that their feet were manacled to a bench.

The cop at the desk was writing in a register. He was a large man, but personable and neatly attired. The Station House Officer, AM Goyal, as the brass name stand on his desk proclaimed. While we were waiting outside the gate, the villagers had related horror stories about him, and I'd fully expected to encounter a beast; but this guy looked like he worked in an MNC.

'What can I do for you?' he asked politely.

The villagers had not followed me inside, but my own men had, and they fanned out in the room. They were tall, fit guys and looked quite intimidating, but he didn't appear to be in the least bit perturbed.

'You're detaining a friend of mine illegally. I want you to release him.'

'What is your friend's name?' he asked.

'Manjeet Singh Walia from Tarn Bali, and his son Ranjeet.'

'I'm sorry, but we can't do that. These men have been picked up for colluding with terrorists.'

'I can vouch for these people. They're innocent farmers. If you have any evidence against them, show me your arrest warrant.'

For the first time he appeared a bit flustered.

'This man you speak of, Manjeet, is the father of a notorious terrorist called Ravinder Singh Walia. We have proof that they are in touch with him. They even provide him with food and shelter when he has nowhere else to run.'

'If this is so, then show me the proof, otherwise release him immediately. Show me the warrant for his arrest, if you have one, or else I am going to take him back with me right now.'

'*Afsar saab*, you should know that this is a police matter and the Army has no right to interfere. The SSP himself has ordered his arrest,' he said, picking up his pen in dismissal.

In hindsight, it was a foolish thing to do, but at the time I couldn't restrain myself. My rage had built up to a boil, and his smug expression was only making it worse.

I reached across the desk, dug my fingers into his collar and lifted him up, towards me. His mug was so close to mine that we were almost French kissing.

'Listen, *madarchod*, did you not understand what I said? I want you to release them *now*, right this minute, or things will not go well for you.'

'Okay,' he croaked, 'okay.' And *now* his voice had a noticeable quaver.

I let go of him and he sank back into his seat. He had a creamy complexion and I could see that his neck had turned blotchy. He pressed a buzzer on his desk and one of the *hawaldars* showed up at the door.

'Get the prisoners,' he said.

Manjeet and his son were escorted into the room and I could see that the old man had been battered. It looked like a rifle butt had made contact with his skull, which was bleeding. The boy's face bore bruises, too, and both of them appeared to be in a heightened state of terror.

I rose to leave and noticed that the men with me were nervous. I guess storming into cop stations and demanding the release of prisoners was not something that happened very often in their army careers.

The SHO called out to me as I was stepping through the doorway.

'*Afsar saab...*'

When I turned around, he was grinning. It was a vicious grin and altered his face completely.

'You will have to pay for this, you know,' he informed me. 'An action like this will have consequences.'

It was a prophetic statement, for both of us, as it turned out.

CHAPTER 29

Almost two weeks had gone by since the incident and I'd begun half-believing that I would get away with it... that that pudgy bastard in his starched uniform had been so intimidated by me that he had let the matter drop. This led me to commit a huge blunder as far as army protocol was concerned, for in hindsight, what I should've done was discussed the matter with my CO, and then requested him to present my case to the Brigadier.

Instead, what played out was that the cops meticulously built up their side of the story, which was later conveyed to the DGP. I'm sure the version he received was a mangled one, but this was a bloke who had a reputation for backing his men to the hilt. Plus, he was highly connected. I came to know later that when he heard about the incident, he was absolutely livid. He got on the phone to the Defence Minister, who, luckily for me, also had a reputation for sticking up for his men. The exercise of power, though, trickled down, and I was summoned for a meeting with Brigadier Singh.

I had had a chat with Kartar and the other chaps who had tagged along and I knew they would back my version of events.

On the appointed day I shaved closely, dabbed on the aftershave, and right on schedule marched into KP Singh's office smelling like a pimp.

My CO Pradhan was already seated inside and he glared at me as if I'd groped his sister. No doubt the Brigadier had already given him his before summoning me.

That was another thing about the army. The CO was responsible for all the troops under his command, especially the officers. A troublemaker like me could easily screw up *his* prospects of rising up the ladder. I knew that, given half a chance, he would shop me, and, quite honestly, I didn't give a fuck. All I wanted was to save the damsel and get the hell out.

***

The Brigadier didn't ask me to sit, which told me that I was really in for it.

The man was a legend, a soldier's soldier. He was extremely tall, and lithe and muscular, even though he had crossed fifty. He had fought in two wars, on the frontlines, and been decorated for bravery. I'd heard that he had been a champion wrestler in his youth and his cauliflower knobs bore testimony to this. This was a gent who could take a beating and still come at you with everything he had.

'You've fucked up big time, officer,' he barked. 'Who gave you the order to barge into a police station like that?'

I remained silent. Long experience of getting told off by seniors had taught me that it was better to let them blow off steam. But this was not my CO, Pradhan.

'I asked you a question, soldier: who gave the order?' He was shouting now.

'No one, sir.'

'No one,' he repeated; 'which means that, without orders, you requisitioned an army jeep, drove to a police station and manhandled the station in charge.'

'Yes, sir.'

He seemed a bit taken aback.

'So, then, why did you do it?'

'Sir, they had picked up a couple of my friends, without an arrest warrant, and they were holding them illegally. Both the man and boy were severely beaten.'

'These so-called *friends* of yours are connected to the insurgency movement. They have a son who is a suspected terrorist, am I correct?'

'Their son, Ravi, left their home a few years ago and has never been seen since. They believe that he has gone abroad, like many Sikh youths do these days.'

'Listen, chappie, are you trying to bullshit me? That boy, Ravinder, has been on the wanted list for a long time now.'

I said nothing.

'Well?' he said.

'Sir, I know this family well. They are decent, law-abiding people. The father retired from the Sikh Regiment. He used to be a nursing assistant and now he runs a free clinic in the village. The boy is only fifteen and he intends to join the army.'

I saw his eyes widen slightly. This piece of info had not been relayed to him.

'Each time there is an incident in the district they are picked up, thrown behind bars and threatened. In the past, the old man was held for over two weeks, without a warrant, and brutally tortured. Every time the DGP pays a visit, or there is pressure from the local SSP, the old man is hauled in as a suspected terrorist... to make up the numbers, in a manner of speaking.'

His tone had softened somewhat when he said, 'I am aware of this, but do you feel that it gives you the right to take the law into your own hands, and malign the reputation of your regiment?'

'No, sir,' I said, and meant it. He was absolutely right, it was a serious offence.

'You will be confined to the base until further notice. Do I make myself clear?' he said.

'Yes, sir,' I replied, knowing that I was being let off lightly.

'Listen, Gabriel, this is a very tricky situation. We're in a difficult place, and it's a godawful time to be here. I am well aware of this. But we're here to do a certain job, and do it we must, whatever be the cost. If we fail, the entire country will pay dearly.'

I nodded.

'Now, to do this job we *need* the Punjab Police. We don't always approve of their methods, but you must admit that they have an in-depth knowledge of the terrain and the people, which we lack. I don't like it either when they target the families of suspected terrorists, but the fact is that it's bloody effective. Nowadays, the youth in the villages think a hundred times before embarking on some foolish crusade. I want you to consider this seriously.'

I had, and I still didn't like it. I said nothing, though; merely saluted smartly and stepped out of his cabin. On my way out, I noticed that my CO had a disappointed expression on his porcine mug, which he was trying hard to conceal.

CHAPTER 30

I was confined to barracks for over a month and assigned a number of menial tasks to perform, courtesy of my prick of a CO. Not that this bothered me too much, as I'd always been cynical of the huge distinctions made between officers and serving men... flotsam from a colonial past that one could do without.

What I did resent, immensely, was my inability to meet Simar.

I used to ring up at the hostel in Amritsar and the first few times she came on the line she seemed distracted and withdrawn. When I called a few weeks later, they informed me that she had gone home.

I tried calling her there, but never got a chance to speak to her. Each time her mum came on the line and informed me, in an increasingly indifferent manner, that Simar was not around, that she'd gone over to a neighbour's place and would call back later. No call ever came through, though.

I had a fair idea of what must have transpired. After the incident at the cop station, the family would have been threatened, and instructed to stay away from me, if they knew what was good for them.

All I wanted was to meet her and explain that things would be okay… that the troubles would end, and then we could get married and live happily ever after.

Ah, the fallacies of youth.

**

Finally, after what seemed like an eternity, I was summoned to the CO's office and granted permission to leave the base. There were to be no further incidents, I was told. I was also advised to keep away from Manjeet's family.

And, of course, the first thing I did was requisition a jeep and drive like a madman through that flat, verdant landscape.

I knew that things would be different, but I had not realised just how much.

I entered the courtyard of their home and parked in my usual spot. In the past, the door would have been thrown open even before I reached the porch, and Ranjeet would be waiting there to embrace me. This time, though, it remained shut.

I pressed the calling bell and waited. After a while, I heard the sound of footsteps padding softly up to the door. It was the old man, Manjeet. It was dark inside and I couldn't make out his expression.

'How are you, uncle?' I asked, and stepped inside.

He turned away from me, muttered something inaudible and limped away.

'What happened?' I asked. 'What crime have I committed that all of you have stopped speaking to me?' I said it in a joking manner, but I was dead serious. Something was not right here. Their home, usually so warm and welcoming, appeared like a tomb to me.

My eyes were getting accustomed to the gloom and it was only after a while that I saw the old lady. She was standing at the entrance to the kitchen and staring at me.

'What happened, aunty*ji*? Why are all of you keeping a distance from me?'

She said nothing for a while, and I could sense the nervousness emanating from her, this lady who had always seemed so fearless to me.

'You must leave, *beta*, and never come back,' she said finally. 'You must go out of our lives forever.'

'But why, aunty? Is it because of the police? Have they threatened you? I'll make sure that it never happens again.'

'*Nooo*,' she yelled, startling me. 'You must *never* do that, do you understand? You must never interfere in our matters again.'

This was grossly unfair. It was she who had called and pleaded for my help.

I was just about to say something when I noticed the old man looking at us. He had paused at the doorway to their bedroom and his face was turned towards me.

Both his eyes were almost completely shut, covered with wads of blue-black tissue. His face appeared drawn and grey in the areas that were not bruised. His mouth hung open and I could see that he had lost most of his teeth. I felt the madness welling up inside, but tried not to show it.

'Who did this to you, uncle?' I said. 'Just give me a name. Who did this to you?'

Before he could answer, the old lady screamed.

'*Leave*,' she said. 'Please get out of our house. *Pleeease...* I'm begging you.'

'Aunty, all I have done is tried to help you. Why are you treating me like this?' My eyes had welled up and I could feel a tear coursing down my cheek.

Her face softened when I said this, and when she spoke her tone was even.

'I know, *beta*, but these are terrible times, you must understand this. Our family is in grave danger. Your presence here will only make it worse. You must leave now and never come back. They will slaughter us all unless you do as I say.'

I should have left like she asked me to, but the hurt and the rage were all-consuming.

'I'm sorry, aunty, but I will need to speak to your daughter first. If Simar asks me to leave then I will, but not before that.'

She appeared to mull over this for a while. My eyes were drawn towards the old man, and it was a pathetic sight. Clad in a faded white *kurta pyjama*, he seemed like a ghost to me. He was looking at me and I noticed a thin stream of liquid trickling down from the one eye he could still see with. Both of us looked away simultaneously.

Finally, the old lady spoke.

'You may talk to her, but you must promise to leave after that.'

I nodded.

'Simar,' she called out, and her daughter stepped out of the kitchen. She had heard every word.

It had been a while since I'd last seen her and I found her presence unnerving. I moved towards her, but she held up a hand to stop me.

'I'm sorry, but you must leave our house immediately,' she said in a listless voice.

I was shocked, more by her tone than what she'd said to me.

'Simi, what are you saying? It's me... Victor.'

Her expression was impassive, but her eyes had filled up. Perhaps I did have a chance, after all.

'Simar, the troubles are going to end, very soon, and then all of this will be behind us. We can make a fresh start somewhere else... not just you and I, but all of us.'

She stared at me in silence, and then, almost imperceptibly, I saw something harden inside her. I braced myself for what I knew was coming.

'All this cannot happen, Victor. Our lives have changed completely. What we once thought was possible cannot happen now. You must leave and never return. If you care for me at all, you will do as I say.'

I was desperate and searching for allies. Besides, something about the situation didn't seem right to me.

'Where is Ranjeet?' I asked.

All three of them were silent, but the mother had begun to weep.

'Where is Ranjeet?' I asked again.

'They have him, Victor,' said Simar.

'Who?'

'The police... that SHO you fought with.'

'But *why*?' I screamed. 'He's just a boy; he hasn't done anything.'

'My father didn't do anything either, and see what they've done to him.'

She was crying now and I moved to comfort her, but once again she raised her hand to stop me.

'How long will they hold him?'

'I don't know, Victor; they keep telling us that he will be released soon.'

I felt a wave of powerlessness wash over me.

'Have they asked you for money?' I said.

Both mother and daughter looked at each other.

'No,' replied the old lady.

'You must leave now, Victor,' said Simar. 'I cannot meet you again.'

I turned around and walked out. As I started up the jeep, I saw that she had come to the window and was staring at me.

***

A few weeks later, I received a call from her mother.

CHAPTER 31

It was late in the evening and I was in the middle of a booze-up with a few close mates when I was summoned to the mess for a phone call. I was pretty sozzled and thought at first that I'd take a pass. It was, in all probability, the chump, also in an inebriated state, calling to check on his only son. He had taken to doing this of late, which I found endearing, though not on this occasion.

I asked the orderly to find out who it was, and he came back saying that there was a lady on the line, speaking in Punjabi and sounding desperate.

As I left the room, there was general ribbing about the Punjabi lady who was so eager to talk to me. I lurched out of my quarters and got into the jeep parked outside.

It was not Simar, as I had hoped, but her mother. She was sobbing on the phone, in a state of near-hysteria.

'What happened, aunty?"

'*Betaaa*,' she wailed, 'come see what they have done to us.'

Ranjeet, I thought, as a sliver of red-hot metal slid into my brain.

'I'm coming,' I said, and put the phone down.

'Sir, I'll come with you,' the orderly offered, and I nodded. I was pretty wasted, and the last thing I needed was a pile-up on the way to the village.

'Don't mention where we are going to anybody,' I ordered.

'Yes, sir,' he replied.

The boy was a good driver and we reached their home in just over an hour. As we pulled in, I saw that a crowd had assembled in the courtyard. Almost the entire village appeared to be there.

Many of the neighbours turned to stare at me. A few of them had accompanied me to the police station and knew how close I was to the family. I saw some of them averting their eyes, which troubled me.

I went inside and the first person I noticed was Ranjeet. His eyes were bloodshot and his face was badly bruised, but in every other way he seemed to be okay. And alive.

As soon as he saw me, he rushed forward and buried his face in my chest.

'What happened?' I asked softly, my dread increasing. 'What did they do to you?'

'Not me,' he croaked, 'Simar.'

I pushed him aside and rushed into his parents' bedroom. She was laid out on the bed and appeared to be sleeping. I could barely make out her face, which was wrapped in a translucent *dupatta*. I moved closer and saw that it was pallid and bloated.

Her mother sat on the bed, surrounded by a group of fierce-looking matrons who were all staring at me. She stood up and came forward, and for a moment I thought she would strike me, but instead she threw her arms around my waist and sobbed into my chest.

I felt the madness consuming me. Someone would pay for this, I knew, with his life at the very least.

'How did it happen?' I asked, wiping away the tears that slid down my cheeks.

'She killed herself, *beta*,' the old lady replied. 'She threw herself into the well.'

The well in their field, where we had kissed for the first time. I felt my legs going and had to sit down on the bed. I had never felt so weak, so helpless.

'Why, aunty? *Why?*' She was in her final semester of the MBBS course and would have been a qualified doctor in less than a year.

I watched her expression harden, and I knew that she would not tell me, not here, not in front of all these people.

'I don't know, *beta*... I don't know why she would ever do such a thing.'

'Where is Manjeet*ji*?'

'They took him to the hospital. He had a stroke shortly after it happened. She had always been his favourite.'

Manjeet's bond with Simar had been even deeper, I knew. She would have become the doctor he had always wanted to be.

***

I sent the orderly back to the base with instructions to inform the folks there that something urgent had cropped up, and that I would resume duties shortly.

My CO, Colonel Pradhan, had already ordered an inquiry into the previous incident. The man was a climber, and he knew that he would go down with yours truly unless he piled up the paper. Not showing up for duty would simply add to this mound, not that I cared overly.

As far as I was concerned, I was done with the army.

Simar's mum was wary and reticent, which was understandable. She'd lost one child to the insurgency, and another, most likely, to the police. Her husband was on his deathbed, and the last thing she wanted was to lose Ranjeet.

I knew this, and so I did not press her. These were a warrior people and in time she would tell me.

Ranjeet was the one who first opened up to me. A few days after the cremation, he and I took a walk to their fields. He sat at the very edge of the stream and stared down at the muddy water, while I lolled on the grass nearby. I could sense that he wanted to share something and waited for him to speak.

'*Bhai*, there is something I need to tell you, but you must promise that you will never repeat this to anyone.'

'Okay,' I said.

'You promise?'

'I give you my word, Ranjeet. Now tell me.'

'*Bhai*, something bad happened to my sister when I was inside… something *very* bad.'

I said nothing.

'When I was in there, she would come to the station every day to plead with them to release me. The SHO would tell me this when they were torturing me.'

'Did they beat you very badly?'

He did not reply, but instead he rolled up a pant leg. His shin was blue and black and lumpy. They had beaten him with a wooden baton, most likely. I felt the fury well up inside, but forced myself to remain calm. There would be time for that later. For the moment, I had to get him to speak.

'One day, they brought Simar to the lock-up to see me. They had just finished a session and I'd been dragged back to my cell. I was lying on the floor, completely naked, when the SHO brought her in, to show her what they'd done to me.

'I didn't know what to do when she came in. The shame was great, but I was in so much pain that I couldn't even cover myself properly. She broke down, right there in the cell, and began screaming. I could see the SHO's face very clearly. He was standing just behind her and smiling down at me.'

His voice had cracked and tears were streaming down his cheeks. I reached forward and held him. He winced as I did this and I could feel his ribs under the T-shirt. This was a boy who had once dreamt of serving his country.

He rested his head against my shoulder for a while and then he pulled away.

'But that was not the worst part, *bhai*. When the SHO led her away, I heard him saying, "The choice is yours, but make it quickly. He will not last in here forever."'

I allowed the hate to boil inside me, and then subside to a simmer. It was better that way, as I could think more clearly.

'Two days later, they released me. Even after I returned home, the calls kept coming. A couple of times a police jeep pulled up outside our house and she went with them. My mother tried to stop her, but she insisted on going.'

Ranjeet turned to stare at me.

'These are very evil men, *bhai*. Now I understand why my brother had to leave.'

CHAPTER 32

A week later, the old man died.

I reached their home in the morning, and she told me that he had gone in his sleep. The entire village turned up for his funeral, plus several folks from the surrounding countryside. There was not a child in the vicinity he hadn't treated, they informed me.

I cornered her a few days after the cremation, when Ranjeet had gone out to meet some friends.

'Aunty, now you must tell me what happened with Simar,' I said, and after a moment's silence she nodded her head.

'It's a shame, *beta*, a terrible shame that such things are allowed to happen in our country,' she began, 'that men like this prosper, while innocent people are hounded and killed.'

'Who are you talking about, aunty?'

Again, there was a pause, before she resumed speaking.

'The SHO at the police station, *beta*... the dog you picked a fight with. At that time, I believed it was foolish on your part, but now I know that it was only my fear speaking. We thought that if we remained silent, he would let us be, but we were so wrong about him. Such people need to be destroyed.'

Her voice was trembling and tears were running down her cheeks.

'I need to know everything,' I said.

And she told me. Slowly and with great effort, over the course of the next few days, during which time I stayed over at their place, absent from duty without permission. It was getting to be a habit with me.

***

There had been a bank robbery in Amritsar, she began, in the course of which the fleeing bandits had gunned down quite a few people indiscriminately. One of these men had apparently matched the description of their elder son, Ravi.

'This was a lie,' she informed me. 'Ravinder was nowhere in the vicinity.'

"How do you know?" I asked. "Do you know where he is?"

She was silent for a while, mulling things over, and then she made up her mind to trust me.

'I don't know where he is, but I have a number I can call when I need to get in touch with him. He comes to see me once in a while.'

'And he told you that he was not involved in this incident?'

'He gave me his word, Bictor, and I believe him. You see, my son is not an ordinary boy. He has always been deeply religious, almost saintly. He would *never* lie to me.'

I didn't know what to believe. She was, after all, a mother defending her son.

'A week after this incident, they came and took my husband away. In the lock-up they beat him so badly that his internal organs were ruptured. Simar and I would go to the station every day and plead with the SHO to release him. He would laugh in our faces and tell us to inform Ravinder to turn himself in.

'For four or five days they tortured him. Then, when he began vomiting blood, they threw him in a jeep and dumped him in front of our house.'

'We thought that they would leave us alone after this, but it was not to be. The very next day he came, in a van this time, filled with policemen, and they dragged Ranjeet away. I tried to stop them, but they threw me to the ground. One of them even kicked me in the stomach as I lay there.

'Over the next few days, he was tortured so brutally that it was a wonder he did not die. They beat him with their fists, hung him from a truck tyre and whipped him with rubber straps and wooden sticks for hours at a stretch. Did he show you the marks?'

I nodded.

'We used to go there every day and plead with that dog Goyal to release him, and he would simply smile and ask us whether we had informed Ravinder about what was happening to his brother.'

'After a few days, he told me that I couldn't come to the station any more and that Simar should come on her own if she wanted to enquire about Ranjeet.

'At first, I refused to let her go, but she insisted. She kept telling me that they would murder him in the lock-up and dispose of the body if we did not make constant enquiries.

'The first couple of times he treated her civilly. Once he even let her go in and see Ranjeet. That night, when she came back, she looked like she was dying, but she didn't say a word to me.

'Later, she told me that he had said she could save him if she wished. That all she had to do was sleep with him. That Ranjeet would be killed like so many others if she did not do this, and we would not even get to see his body.'

I was surprised at my own response to this. I did not once break down, nor go into a rage; instead, I remained calm all through the telling.

'She told me that he took her to a lodge in Amritsar and raped her repeatedly. When she came back home, she locked herself up in her room and did not step out for several hours. And the very next day they released Ranjeet.'

'Did she kill herself after this?'

'No, not immediately. What happened was that, even after this, the calls kept coming and she would be summoned to the station, or somewhere else. And now it wasn't only that dog who was doing it — even his superiors were in on it. Usually, it was Goyal's jeep that was sent to fetch her, but once another car came, which, my neighbour informed me, belonged to the SSP.'

By now she had broken down completely.

'Oh, the shame, *beta*, the *shame*. How can I ever live with myself? *I* allowed her to do it. I, who could have stopped her... or asked Ravi to surrender. Only I have his number, and he would have listened to me... but I wanted to save my son. Oh, the shame, the shame,' she wailed.

I waited until the crying had subsided. She was breathing heavily and there was a heaving, gasping sound emanating from her chest.

'Aunty, I want Ranjeet and you to leave this place for a while. Do you have anywhere to go outside Punjab, preferably even further away than Delhi?'

She stared at me for a while.

'I have a nephew in Bombay... we can stay with him,' she said finally.

'Good. Make the arrangements.'

She nodded.

'And now please make the call, aunty. I would like to speak to Ravi.'

CHAPTER 33

Ravi was a tall lad, much taller than me, and unlike what I'd expected. I had conjured up an image of a younger Bhindranwale, but aside from the height and lanky build, there were few similarities.

He was good-looking in a boyish way, almost like a caricature of his sister. The growth on his face was sparse and straggly and he had a prominent Adam's apple which bobbed up and down when he spoke. At first, I found myself wondering if he'd serve my purpose, but I needn't have worried on that score.

Callow as he seemed, our boy was a pro.

***

A few weeks after her husband's death, I received the call from Simar's mother.

Later, I found out that setting up a meeting with her elder son was a laborious process. The old lady had taken a bus to a neighbouring town, from where she'd made a call from a PCO. She returned home that evening and rang up to inform me that she was organizing a *puja* for her husband and that she wanted me to attend. This was a code we had set up to communicate that Ravi would be coming that night.

I arrived at their home a few hours later and she welcomed me warmly, even though the strain on her face was evident. Ranjeet was there, too, but he didn't know why I had come. After dinner, she asked me to rest for a while as Ravi usually showed up in the middle of the night. I napped for a bit till she woke me, and then rose quickly, splashed water on my face and walked into the hall.

There were four of them, all Sikhs, and they rose to their feet when they saw me.

'This is the boy I told you about,' the old lady said to the youngest man in the group, 'the one Simar would have married.' I felt a lump in my throat and tears welled up, which I tried to suppress.

The one she would have married.

He moved towards me and the others followed, forming a semi-circle around us.

'*Paaji*, I'm sorry,' he said, before hugging me. I could see that his eyes were red and that he'd been crying. All of them embraced me, one after the other, almost ceremoniously. Not one of them, I knew, was a stranger to loss.

We talked into the wee hours of the morning, undisturbed, as the old lady had bolted the door of Ranjeet's room from the outside. She told me that she did this whenever Ravi visited. Ranjeet had no clue that his long-lost sibling was an occasional caller at their home.

The old lady, her son and I sat some distance away from the others. My misgivings regarding Ravinder had vanished. He was quite young, a couple of years younger than I, but the manner in which he carried himself was impressive. This was a man who was born to lead... a man you crossed at your peril.

For over an hour he spoke about his sister, their growing-up years, and how close they'd been. Simar had made him promise that he would attend her wedding, wherever and whenever it was held. His face was stony when he said this, although his mother was weeping and my eyes had filled up as well. I realised that all of them had accepted me as a part of their family, the son-in-law to be.

He had an AK-56 which was placed on the sofa beside him, and I wondered where he'd got it. I'd never seen such a piece in the regular Indian Army.

After a while, the old lady rose, went into the kitchen and returned with tea and snacks for all of us. The men dug in with gusto. Ravi fished around in his carry bag and came up with a wad of notes, which he placed in her hand.

'You will need to stay in Bombay for at least a few years, *bebe*,' he said.

She nodded mutely.

'Make sure that Ranju attends a very good school,' he went on. 'I will arrange for the money.'

Once again, she nodded.

'Bring him up as an Amritdhari Sikh,' he intoned, more *sant* than son to her. 'I will send for you once the troubles have ended.'

She broke down and sobbed, probably realising that she would never see this son again. He rose to his feet and she got up, too, and they hugged each other.

'Go inside and sleep now. You will not see me for some time, but you must pray for me, and for all of us.'

She did as he said, wordlessly.

When she had gone, he sat down again, and the other three, who had been sitting apart, clustered around us.

CHAPTER 34

Back at the base, I went through my daily routine in a state of nervousness and anticipation, waiting for a call that I knew would come.

I'd expected to receive it within a couple of days, but almost a fortnight had passed since the meeting with Ravi. I knew, though, that several issues needed to be sorted out. Ranjeet and his mother would have to leave the state, intel had to be garnered, weapons arranged for and the right men chosen to do the job. Targeting a senior police officer, even in Punjab, was a serious matter.

I knew that Ravi would never back down. I had seen it in his eyes. But perhaps he had decided to exclude me from the operation. Perhaps he felt I was too great a risk to take along.

If this happened, I knew that one part of me would be secretly relieved, but at the same time I *wanted* to be there, to make sure it was properly done. Experienced as these chaps were, such actions had a very high chance of getting botched up. I'd seen it happen in the past.

Finally, just as I was beginning to think that I'd read about it in the papers, I received a phone call. It was Simar's mother on the line, enquiring whether I could come over the next morning.

***

When I entered the compound, I saw that they were all packed and ready to leave. A number of suitcases and satchels were strewn on the porch, and Ranjeet and I loaded these in the jeep, while she bade goodbye to the neighbours.

At Amritsar station, I waited with the old lady on the platform, while Ranjeet entered the second-class compartment and stowed the luggage under their seats. There was an air of maturity about him that had not been there earlier.

Just before his mother boarded, she held my face in both hands.

'He asked me to tell you that it would be very soon, *beta*. He said that a woman would call, and that you should be ready.'

I nodded. She then kissed me on both cheeks and got into the train. I waved at Ranjeet, who was staring at me through a barred window.

***

The call finally came almost a month after they had left. A husky voice on the other end of the line urged me to meet up with her that evening in a restaurant opposite the train station in Amritsar. She sounded overly flirtatious on the phone, which I suppose was to throw off potential eavesdroppers.

I arrived early and hung around the area, trying to spot her. Failing to do so, I stepped into the restaurant at the allotted hour and ordered a cup of tea.

She came and sat down on the bench next to me. Her manner was confident, even brazen, which was perfectly fine with me.

'If anyone asks tell them that you spent the entire night with me.'

'Where do you stay?' I asked.

She pointed upward, indicating the floor above the restaurant. Her eyes were staring into mine and she was flirting with me. Perhaps it was the proximity of danger, but I found her wildly attractive.

'Maybe I'll come and see you again, after all this is over,' I said.

She burst out laughing.

'You really think you could?'

I smiled and nodded.

'That would be nice. I would like that very much,' she said.

'How do you know these people?' I asked, after a while, just to keep the conversation going.

'No more questions,' she replied; 'they'll be here soon.'

Almost immediately, we heard the sound of loud honking outside the restaurant.

'They're here,' she informed me, suddenly nervous.

'I'll be back soon; wait up for me,' I said, and she smiled and nodded.

***

My escorts turned out to be a bunch of flashily dressed youths in an open jeep with *bhangra* music blaring loudly.

They greeted me warmly enough, but once we were on our way none of them said anything more to me. They resumed conversing in Punjabi and I strained my ears to pick up what they were saying. From what I could gather, there was a lot of bragging going on, and all of them, including the driver, appeared to be drunk. I was hoping that this was not the crew Ravi had chosen for the job.

We were moving in an easterly direction, but, aside from this, I couldn't make out much. They must've trusted me, though, as they didn't attempt to blindfold me. Either that or I wasn't making the trip back to Amritsar.

We had been driving for over an hour when finally, we pulled up outside one of those ubiquitous *dhabas* that dot the countryside in Punjab.

Ravi was there, waiting for me, and this time around he seemed quite intimidating. He was with a group of five men who were very different from the boys sent to fetch me. They were older, larger and more restrained, and they treated Ravi with a great deal of deference.

I found myself hugely conflicted. These men, I was sure, formed part of an elite squad, trained and motivated foot soldiers in a self-styled holy war being waged against the country.

I saw Ravi handing over a wad of notes to one of the youths who had brought me. He folded his hands in gratitude and then all of them got back into their jeep and disappeared in the direction we had come from.

'*Sat sri akal, paaji,*' Ravi greeted me after they had left.

'*Sat sri akal,*' I replied.

'It is good that you have come, but you needn't have, you know. Either way, you will read about it in the newspapers.'

'I had to... for me, too, this is a matter of honour,' I said, and he nodded. This was a man who knew about honour.

'Get ready,' he addressed his men, who were lounging around on nearby cots, 'it's time to leave.'

The squad rose as one and reached for their weaponry. They appeared better equipped than even the Special Forces in the Indian Army. No wonder the police, with their ancient .303s, had come off so badly in this conflict.

'Ravi,' I said, as we were walking towards his jeep, 'there is something I have to let you know. When this is over, I will still be an army officer, and I will come after you, if they send me.'

'*If* they send you,' he smiled.

'Where are we going?' I asked.

'The dog we are after has a mistress who lives not far from here. Tonight, he will be spending the night with her. We will get him there.'

'Have you been tracking him for a long time?'

I saw his eyes, and even in the darkness they scared me.

'Only after Simar's death. My mother did not tell me till much later... otherwise all of this would not have happened.'

'What about the others... the SSP who ordered the arrest of your father?' I asked.

'We will get them all, one by one, all the way up to Gill*saab*. *Raj karega Khalsa*.'

The age-old war cry of the Sikhs. The Khalsa will rule.

But I knew that this would not happen. As rabid as the insurgents were about claiming their independence, there were far greater numbers of Sikhs, like DGP Gill, who were equally fanatical about preserving the sanctity of the Indian Union. And men like Ravi had lost control of their revolution. It had passed into the hands of brigands and miscreants, who were amassing wealth and wreaking destruction in the name of a freedom struggle. They had lost the moral advantage years ago in the eyes of the nation, and now even the local citizenry was turning against them.

I did not contradict him, though. The last thing I needed was to get into a political debate with him. There was a job to be done, I would help him to do it, and then I planned to get the hell out of there.

**

After around half an hour of driving, we reached a farmhouse situated in the middle of wheat fields. This had to be one self-assured lady, I thought, to carry on an affair with a marked policeman out in the middle of nowhere.

'Who is this woman?' I asked.

'She's the wife of a local *dus numbri*,' Ravi replied, using the Hindi term for a repeat offender.

'He's in jail, and the SHO makes sure he stays alive, as long as she keeps herself available for him.'

'She's supposed to be a real firecracker,' put in one of the men. 'They say she used to be a famous *mujrewali*.'

***

We parked some distance away and moved towards the house in silence. The men had fanned out and we approached from different directions. They appeared to know what they were doing, which reassured me somewhat.

I slipped on my leather gloves and clutched my service revolver tightly. The hate was burning a hole in me, but I was also extremely nervous. What we planned on doing was to commit cold-blooded murder, and there were so many things that could go wrong.

We paused around fifty metres from the house and waited till the driver and bodyguard were taken out. The police jeep was parked in the glow emanating from the porch, and I witnessed this clearly from where I was crouched.

The cops had, in all likelihood, made the trip several times before, as they were dozing in the vehicle. I watched as Ravi's men slipped their *kirpans* back into their scabbards and gestured to us to approach.

'These are good men,' I said to Ravi.

'The very best,' he replied. 'All of them fought alongside Sant Bhindranwale. They escaped from the Harmandir Sahib just before the army atrocities commenced.'

I said nothing. If that was what he chose to believe, then so be it. To sustain a conflict of this nature, you needed something to fuel the hatred.

We passed the jeep as we crept up to the house and I could see that both the driver and guard were slouched forward, one on the wheel and the other on the dashboard. I was on the side closer to the steering wheel and I saw blood dripping to the floor. The man's neck had been almost severed from his torso and his head rested on the wheel at an awkward angle.

I suppressed a shudder. These were hard men and it was in my interest to let them believe that I was made no different.

This SHO was either very desperate or a fool, I thought. To move around the countryside at night in an official vehicle without a sizeable escort was inviting trouble.

I saw Ravi gesture to one of the men, who crept up onto the porch, fished out what looked like a wire and began picking the lock. He was good at it, for in less than a minute he had the door open.

Five of us trooped in, while the remaining two waited outside. I had asked Ravi about the possibility of there being guard dogs, and he'd replied that there had been a dog, but it'd been poisoned a week back.

The operation had been planned to a nicety. They even knew the room in which the lady slept. As we moved towards her bedroom, I noticed that the house was nicely furnished. There was a colour television and an expensive-looking music system in the hall.

Guess it paid to put out for the police in these parts.

CHAPTER 35

The turd was busy pounding away when we barged in.

The lights came on, and for a moment they turned into statues right in the middle of their rutting. It was like one of those Renaissance works, though nowhere near as awe-inspiring.

The room was quite large and as we moved towards the bed I could see the men leering at the woman. She was naked and had pendulous breasts, which swung freely as she tried to sit up.

'Cover yourself,' snarled Saint Ravinder, while his men gaped. He and I were the only ones not gawking at her melons. She pushed the cop off her hurriedly and wrapped herself in a blanket. She then crouched on the ground on the far side of the bed and gazed at us in soundless terror.

I think they knew that there would be no redemption, but sometimes hope can be a terrible thing.

Goyal's penis had shrunk into a flaccid little protrusion, barely visible beneath the girth of his belly. Ravi moved towards him and I followed.

'Do you know who I am?' Ravi asked in a mild tone.

'No... no, sir,' the SHO stammered.

Ravi's arm moved with a swiftness that belied his manner. It caught the SHO on the nose and turned his face into a bloody mess. Like many Sikhs, he, too, knew how to use his *kada* in a fight.

Goyal fell back, snivelling. He had recognised me and his cop brain would've figured out the identity of the boy who stood in front of him.

'My name is Ravinder Singh Walia, from Tarn Bali. I believe you know my family, especially my sister, Simarjeet.'

'No, sir, I swear I don't know any Simarjeet. There's been a mistake. Maybe you're looking for another officer. I'll help you to locate him, I swear,' he wailed. Gone was the composure I'd witnessed in the cop station.

Ravi's fist snaked out and I saw a thick welt rising up on the forehead of the policeman. The boy could hit, that was for sure.

'Stand him up,' he said quietly, and two of the men lifted up the SHO by his shoulders. Ravi was no longer just a gangly youth in an oversized *kurta*. There was a menace about him that was truly frightening.

'Do you know who this man is?' Ravi asked, pointing at me. 'This is the man who was supposed to wed my sister… my only sister, who you raped and then murdered.'

'Sir, I did not kill her, I swear. In fact, I tried to help her. I was the one who got your father and brother released.'

'And were you not the one who put them inside first?' Ravi asked.

The SHO did not reply. He was blubbering now, and it was disgusting to see. I wanted this to be over.

Ravi was not done with him, though.

'Did you know she was studying to be a doctor?'

Goyal was staring at the floor, muttering something under his breath.

'Did you know, I asked,' screamed Ravi. I had never witnessed such fury.

'Yes,' the SHO replied.

'Did you know that my father served in the Indian army? That he fought in two wars for *your* country? And still you tortured him to death.'

'Sir, we had our orders... we were only doing what our superiors instructed.'

'Your superiors instructed you to rape my sister?' Ravi asked, and, as if by magic, a *kirpan* appeared in his hand.

'Sir, please, sir, I have a wife and three daughters. Please not this, sir. I will do anything you ask. Name your price and I will pay it.' He sounded hysterical now.

'Hold him,' Ravi said, and his men tightened their grips. Their lips were retracted in feral grins.

I was watching them and so I didn't see Ravi's hand move, or maybe I looked away. What I did see was the cop's face contorting in a scream, which then subsided into a gurgle. His mouth opened and closed like a fish washed up on shore.

Ravi was holding up something which looked like a small lump of gristle. The SHO had slumped to the ground and was trying to stem the blood flowing out from between his legs.

Ravi flung his genitals on his face and then turned towards me.

'Do what you came here to do,' he said, handing me his revolver. 'We don't have much time.'

I knew why he wanted me to pull the trigger. Goyal was a senior officer on the force and there were bound to be repercussions.

I took the gun from him and, as I raised it, the woman started moaning. One of the men crossed over and clouted her on the head with the butt of his rifle. The SHO was whimpering, but making no further attempts to bargain with us. The only thing he could hope for now was a speedy end.

I could see all of them watching me, wondering if I'd go ahead with it. Strangely, I felt nothing at all. This was a creature who deserved to be killed, and it was up to me to do it. I thrust the pistol into his mouth and squeezed the trigger, and blood and brain matter cascaded onto the far wall like an abstract painting.

'Mumma,' a voice said, and we all spun around.

She must've been four or five years old and looked like an angel. She had dark brown curls, a snub nose and eyes that were grey and serious. She had walked into the room on hearing the sounds, and she didn't know what was happening.

'Where is my Mumma? Who are you?' she asked me in Punjabi.

The woman had regained consciousness and began screaming.

'*Nooooo*, Sonu, go back to your room. Go back to your room, *now*.'

Another pistol had appeared in Ravinder's hand. I lunged at him, but by then it was too late. The sound of the gunshot reverberated around the room. The child crumpled to the floor, one half of her head blown away.

I leapt at Ravi, held him by the throat and lifted him off the floor, which, of course, was a foolish thing to do. Two of his men grabbed at my arms and pulled me off. They would have shot me if Ravi hadn't stopped them.

They dragged me out of the room and I heard a scream and another gunshot.

***

'I'm very sorry, *paaji*, but these things cannot be helped,' Ravi told me on the way back. 'We are fighting a war and there are bound to be casualties, sometimes women and children as well. If we had let them go, it would have compromised the whole operation. Never forget that what you have committed is cold-blooded murder, and that, too, of a senior police officer.'

I sat in silence all the way back to Amritsar. A few miles from the city, I was instructed to get into another vehicle, which they told me would drop me off at the railway station. I was to go back to the restaurant and spend the night there.

'*Paaji*,' Ravinder said, as he bade goodbye to me, 'you are a brave man and I respect you. In another time and place, we might have been brothers.'

I did not reply.

There were two Sikhs in the van that drove me back to Amritsar. Both of them were silent all through the journey, perhaps sensing my mood.

'You can spend the night in my room,' she said, when I entered the restaurant. I nodded my thanks and climbed a steep flight of stairs at the back of the building. It was a small room, with a bed just large enough to accommodate two people. There was no ventilation and the heat was oppressive. I got out of my clothes and lay down in my briefs.

She came up the stairs a short while later and I listened to the sound of clothes rustling as she undressed.

I lay on my side, at the very edge of the mattress, closed my eyes and pretended to be asleep.

***

It was past noon when I made it back to the base, and by then the bodies had been discovered.

I barely had time to slip into my uniform when I heard a knock on the door. Pradhan's adjutant was waiting outside. He had two men with him.

'The CO wants to see you immediately.'

'Okay, just give me a few minutes. I need to take a dump and a shave,' I replied.

'He said *immediately*, Gabriel,' the officer replied.

The fool was pacing about in his office when I walked in and he stopped in mid-stride when he saw me.

'Where the fuck were you last night, Gabriel?' he asked, trying to sound intimidating.

'I went to Amritsar, sir.'

'How the fuck did you just take off to Amritsar?'

'On my bike, sir.'

He paused. It wasn't going the way he'd wanted.

'Don't give me any of your lip, boy. You're in a massive spot of trouble, and it's going to get worse, I can promise you. Do you fucking understand me?'

I nodded. I had never heard him using an expletive before, and the effort was telling on him.

'So where were you, then?'

'I spent the night with a lady friend. She runs a restaurant right opposite the train station.'

'You expect me to believe this bullshit?'

'Yes, sir.'

***

And, of course, the matter didn't end there.

Pradhan didn't believe me, but there was little he could do about it, as my alibi checked out. Ravi had been careful on that score. The woman he'd chosen was a seasoned professional, and she had an axe to grind as well. Her kid brother, who had gone to attend the martyrdom celebrations of Guru Arjan Singh, had been slain during Operation Blue Star and subsequently branded a terrorist. There was no way she would be turning me in.

But the pressure from above was relentless.

They didn't really want the truth to come out, as it would destroy the army's credibility, but they also couldn't risk having me around.

Pradhan tried to get me on desertion, but the Brigadier intervened and they applied the lesser charges of absence without leave and dereliction of duty, for leaving the base without permission.

The court-martial was conducted speedily, and I co-operated at every juncture.

At the end of it, I was cashiered, chucked out on my arse, and everyone, including yours truly, was greatly relieved.

CHAPTER 36

Ennui had given way to a feeling of loss that was acutely palpable. I found myself overwhelmed by a sense of emptiness and desolation.

Ana, too, was quiet as we headed to the bars that lined the beach. We both knew that there was no going back to the way things used to be.

'Where do you want to go, Vic?' she asked.

'Anywhere is fine with me,' I replied. My funds were depleted, and she would be the one settling the tab.

'Parry's?'

'Sure,' I smiled. 'Why not?'

'The scene of your greatest triumph,' she teased.

'Not mine, Johnny Young's... he's the one who scored that night.'

'You sure?' she asked.

'Didn't you notice how Jazz was walking in Panjim?'

'Eeeyewwww... *gross*,' she said, and punched me, and I lifted her up onto my shoulders and carried her all the way to Parry's.

It was a Sunday evening and not as crowded as the other night, and we got a table at the back, quite close to the beach.

'There's something very sensual about pool players,' I said, pointing to three guys at a nearby table, at least two of whom could put a woman off sex forever.

'Maybe from a guy's perspective,' Ana said. 'Give me a footballer any day.'

'Just think about it... the way those gents are handling their cues... doesn't it remind you of a matador about to go in for the kill?'

'It reminds me of a slob, oversized toothpick in hand, lunging for the last sausage on the plate.'

I burst out laughing, and the slob holding the oversized toothpick turned around and gave me a look.

There were two of them, washed-out *goras*, that is, pitted against the local talent. The Goan kid was a pro, and he was hustling them. I'd watched him play the other night and his game was several notches above the performance he was turning in now.

Of the two guys taking turns to play him, one was so obese he was a cardiac arrest waiting to happen. This fella had a foul mouth, which was working nonstop, especially when he was getting creamed. The bloke with him was quieter, but looked like a thug: squat, muscular, with a shaven pate and all.

They were playing for high stakes by Goan standards: five hundred a game. The boy was letting them pick up one in three, though he could've beaten them ten out of ten, and easily.

We sat there watching and as the drinks began going in, the fat guy became even more voluble. The insults turned crasser and were now openly racist as well. The boy didn't appear to mind — perhaps he was used to the score — but it was starting to piss me off like hell. Ana, too, seemed visibly upset.

'Hey, buddy,' I called out, 'you really ought to calm down. There are ladies present, so mind the language.'

They turned to give me the stare-down.

'You talking to *me*?' Blubberbutt said, and it was classic *Taxi Driver*, only this time coupled with *The Nutty Professor*.

'Yes, Travis, I'm talking to you.'

'Why don't you just sit there and mind your own business, arsehole.'

Ana had her hand on my forearm and I pushed it away as I got to my feet.

I gave him the look, the blank one, and I saw him losing his bottle even before I spoke.

'That's exactly what I was doing, all this while, fucker, until you began mouthing off about my country.'

He was throwing nervous glances at the hard man by his side, but that gent didn't want to get involved. He appeared to be Russian, or Eastern European. In those days, there weren't that many of them around.

'Now, are you going to shut that fucking mouth of yours, or do you want me to come over and do it for you?'

'Hey what is your problem, man, we didn't mean any offence.'

'I asked you a simple question, sir. Are you going to pipe down, or should I make you?'

The boy was grinning at me. He'd had a good thing going, but this was even better.

'C'mon, Vlad, we don't need this shit. We come to this godforsaken country to have some fun, and this is what they throw at us.'

'You ought to lighten up, mate,' he said, on his way out.

'So I've been told,' I replied.

This time, even Ana was on my side. She seemed thrilled by what had gone down, even though she abhorred violence. That's the thing about national slurs, they're very unifying.

'My hero,' she simpered, and we both had a laugh.

***

It was techno night in Parry's and the soulless, staccato beat was getting on my nerves. The good thing, though, was that the music was just loud enough to discourage conversation.

Domingo was manning the bar and he winked at me and made incomprehensible gestures as he worked. There was a whole monologue going on in mime, none of which I understood. The place had begun filling up and he was in demand.

I'd just about made up my mind to go over and chat with him when Marge and Jazz waltzed in.

Jazz was clearly a lady who enjoyed turning men on. She was wearing a tight halter top which showed off her boobs, and a white skirt that stopped above mid-thigh. She was a bit too pudgy to carry off the skirt, but the overall effect was stunning.

I didn't notice what Marge had on, not that it mattered. She appeared delighted enough to have spotted Ana, and both of them walked up to our table.

'Wow, we're so glad to see you here. We thought you'd have taken off to somewhere a bit more romantic.'

'What's more romantic than Parry's,' I said, and Jazz burst out laughing, like it was the funniest thing she'd ever heard.

'Hey, Jazz, you missed this guy who was in here just a while back; right, Ana?' I said.

'He was really something, babe. I would have walked out with him, if Vic hadn't physically restrained me.'

'Ana's taken, but he would have been perfect for you,' I said, and Ana burst out giggling.

Jazz wasn't fazed in the slightest. She was one of those women who could gauge instinctively when things were not right with a couple. She sat facing me and was doing things with her eyelashes that were pretty distracting. She had also moved her feet forward until they were brushing against mine. When she slipped off her sandals and began running her toes up my shin, I bailed.

'All right,' I announced, rising from my seat, 'what are you ladies having?'

'Sit down, Vic,' Ana said; 'they'll serve us at the table.'

'Nah,' I replied, 'it's taking too much time. Besides, I'll just go over and say hi to Domingo.'

Domingo looked like he was eager to chat, but the joint was filling up fast and the orders were pouring in.

'I saw the *panja* match with that black bugger, men,' he said after a while, and I thought about a pot and a kettle. 'You're a strong fucker... you go to a gym or what?'

'Used to... years ago.'

Back then I had preferred to hit the weight rooms rather than partake in the running, crawling, marching stuff. I hadn't done it in a while, though.

Domingo droned on, between fixing drinks, about how he was trying to build up his own body.

'Chicks like that shtuff, men; they just love the buff buggers.' Which made sense, of course. At his age, everything was measured in what helped you to score... not that he was doing too badly on that front.

'You should stay away from those other guys, men, that David Colaco and gang,' he said, during our next interaction.

'Who's David Colaco?'

'That fucker with the blue Pajero. He's a slimy bastard, but with solid pull. His pop *runs* the fucking government here.'

'Okay,' I mouthed, not knowing what else to say. I was touched by his concern, though.

After a while I headed back to our table, drinks in hand.

The girls were having an animated discussion about men and marriages and post-marital sex, which I tuned out of. I was hoping that someone interesting would join us, perhaps even a local legend like Johnny Young.

Something had definitely transpired that night between Jazz and Johnny. When I steered the conversation around to the events of that evening, she began squirming, until Marge stepped in and changed the subject. Ana, as usual, knocked her knee against my thigh repeatedly.

CHAPTER 37

I was gazing at the entrance, hoping for the action to pick up, when I saw him walking in. This time around the hat was missing, and his entourage was different, except for the muscle-bound prick, who remained ensnared in his fishing net.

I don't know what it was that drove me to do it, whether it was the *feni*, the grief or the boredom, but I raised my hand and called out to him.

'David,' I shouted above the din, 'over here, bro.'

He looked at me and I saw the nervousness playing on his face. Then he relaxed and his expression reverted to its habitual sneer.

He strode up to our table, followed by his crew, who seemed a lot harder than the chumps he'd been with earlier. Amongst them was an African bloke named Steve, Baby Steve they called him, who might even have given our Johnny a run for his money in the brawn department.

You couldn't fault Davy overly, though, I mused, except for being an arsehole. I would've turned out just as bad, or probably worse, if I'd had as much money. All he seemed to be doing was hanging out with dicks and eyeing women who would always be out of his league. He wasn't even that much of a drinker. As far as I could remember, he'd been sipping on a single drink all through the evening: some weird-looking concoction with an umbrella sticking out of it.

'Wassup, dude?' he said, clasping my hand and giving me a hug. The rest of the guys followed suit, as if we were long-lost mates who'd just caught up. It was a sequence that kept playing out in Goa.

I glanced across at Ana and saw that she was both nervous and upset, and only then did I begin to question what I'd done. It was a bit too late for second thoughts, though, as my newly acquired best buddy had plonked himself down at our table, right next to Jazz, who seemed quite happy to see him.

'So, what are you guys drinking? The next round is on me,' he announced grandly.

Jazz was warming up to him, though both Marge and Ana seemed pissed off. He wasn't a bad-looking dude, I thought charitably, and he could be moderately charming, when he wasn't being an arsehole, that is.

'So, what is it that you do, luv?' Jazz purred in her Brit accent. This turned out to be the wrong question, as he droned on and on about his varied businesses, his cars, his houses and his brand-new twin-engine Cessna.

One would've thought (or hoped) that such kind of talk would put off women, but it wasn't the case I realised when I saw how Jazz was responding. Ana, though, was predictably revolted, and I had to nudge her thigh every once in a while, to let her know we were on the same side.

After a while of this, both Ana and Marge tuned out completely and began conversing amongst themselves, while Jazz, like a thirsty kitten, lapped up all the male attention.

A few drinks down the road (all of which he paid for), she was flirting with him blatantly. She had her arm around his and every once in a while, she rested her head on his shoulder. She was also giggling inanely at everything he said, as if he was the wittiest fella on the planet. Every once in a while, though, I would catch her stealing a glance at me, which I couldn't be bothered to decipher.

The truth was that I was past the point of caring. The only thing running through my head like an insane riff was that, in all probability, it was the last evening Ana and I would spend together.

***

Maybe it was the drinks, or Ana's subtle indifference after our talk, or perhaps it was the arsehole seated in front of me, bragging about all the things I would never have, but all of a sudden, I felt miserable.

I excused myself, walked over to the bar and ordered another *feni*. Given the state of my finances, I was in no position to spring for drinks for everyone at our table, and I didn't need any more of his generosity.

I shot the breeze with Domingo for a while, intermittently, though, as our boy was busy fixing drinks. Most of the time, however, I just stared out at the blackness beyond the shack. The sea was there, and I tried to tune into it, but the sound blaring out of the speakers made this impossible.

All of a sudden, I felt a hand on my chest. Ana had wriggled her way through the crowd and was standing right next to me.

'What's the matter, Vic? What happened?'

It was only then I realised that my eyes had filled up. She came into my arms and clung to me. Up until that moment, I'd always been the stronger one.

'Tell me what happened,' she said again.

'I will, darling, but not here.'

'Let's go back to the room, Vic. I don't want to be here any more.'

'Please stay, Ana, just for a while, and then we'll head somewhere quieter.'

She held me close as I sipped my drink.

'Johnny's going to be majorly pissed off if he walks in here,' I said, nodding at our table.

There were at least four guys surrounding Jazz, seated very close to her, as far as I could make out. The rich prick was sitting astride the bench and she had backed into the space between his thighs. He had his arms around her waist and was stroking her tummy. She was giggling at something he was whispering into her ear. Marge sat forlornly in a corner, excluded from the gaiety.

'Hey, Marge,' I called out.

She looked up and in a second had risen from her seat. I guess she had noticed us canoodling and didn't want to disturb us. There was relief on her face as she moved towards the bar counter.

'She's my kid sister, but she's also such a *slut*,' Marge fumed, after I had jostled around and made space for her. 'It's the same old story wherever we go. By the end of the evening she'll have an army of arseholes pawing at her.' And here I'd been thinking I was kind of special and all.

'Let her be, Marge,' Ana said; 'the babe's on holiday, she's allowed to let her hair down.' The fount of Ana's tolerance probably sprung from the fact that the Jazzter wasn't hitting on me.

My mood had begun to perk up slightly. The girls had gone into a huddle and I found myself chatting with a young couple from Belgium who were standing next to me. They'd spent three weeks trekking through the Himalayas, and had come down to Goa for some R&R before catching a bus to Puttaparthi to meet the Sai Baba.

'Do you believe in him?' the girl queried, with a wide-eyed innocence that could only have come from a privileged background.

'No, but I think my girlfriend does,' I replied, nodding at Ana.

Which didn't count for much, as Ana and her mum had, at one time or the other, been disciples of just about every godman south of the Vindhyas.

'You guys are so fortunate,' she said wistfully.

'How so?' I asked, genuinely curious.

'You know, being Indian and all. You folks are so in touch with your spiritual selves.'

I nodded, feigning interest. Give me spirits over spirituality any day of the week.

On my other side, Ana and Marge had plunged into yet another heart-to-heart. The topic had shifted from Marge's marital woes to career options for Ana. Marge was persuading her to try her luck in the UK, and Ana seemed to be giving it some serious thought.

I looked across at our table, where I could barely see Jazz from where we were standing. The crowd had moved in around her and I wondered if she was okay. To most tourists, Goa appears to be a paradise, but it has another face.

I called out her name from across the room and both Ana and Marge stopped talking.

'Just checking to see if she's all right,' I said, pointing at the mob surrounding her.

The music was blaring, my head was spinning with all the *feni*, and I knew I was being paranoid.

Marge didn't think so, however.

'Jazz,' she screamed above the din in a voice like cannon fire, and I guess this was a pitch her sister was used to, as she immediately surfaced amongst a sea of bobbing heads.

'Yeah?' she screamed back.

'You all right, luv?' Marge asked.

'Yeah,' she replied.

The former cowpoke got up, too, to see what all the fuss was about. His demeanour had changed and there was something about the guy that made me want to stomp on his nuts. I should've done it the other night when I had the chance.

I turned back to the bar before the hate began welling up.

'So, how's it going?' I asked Domingo. 'Any luck so far?'

He grinned at me and nodded.

'You see those two over there?'

I turned to have a look. There were two white girls huddled in a corner with some locals. They appeared to be around sixteen or so.

'Just last night, men, I was with the one in the pink skirt.' He pointed discreetly at the prettier girl.

'How do you do it, buddy? It can't be easy, right? Is it the perfume you're wearing?' He'd been working the bar for several hours and I could get the stench from where I stood.

He started getting all animated, and I was glad Ana wasn't part of this conversation.

'No, men, it's really simple, believe me. See, after some time they'll come up to the bar and start flirting with me, for free drinks, shooters and stuff, and once in a while I'll pour them something. By the end of the evening they're so fucking sloshed they don't know what they're doing. They begin hitting on anyone, even a guy like me.'

It didn't appear as if the previous night had been memorable for the girl in question, as she seemed to be ignoring him completely. Or perhaps she didn't even recognise him. It wasn't that uncommon in places like this.

***

The music was thumping and the room had begun spinning. I'd been drinking for four hours straight and the *feni* and the grief had got hold of me. I clung on to the bar to steady myself.

I felt sick and didn't want to be there any more. I wanted to be alone with Ana, not in our cruddy room, but somewhere quiet and romantic, where we could have a meaningful conversation on our last night together.

I turned to her and said, 'You want to head back, sweetheart? I need to finish packing for tomorrow.'

She smiled. Usually, she was the one who had to drag me away, even after the lights had been dimmed down.

'Of course,' she replied.

Our bill arrived, and it turned out to be a measly figure, a parting gift from Domingo. Ana settled it and gave our barkeep a peck on the cheek.

'I'll see you the next time I'm here,' she said to him.

'You and I, we *must* party together,' Marge said, trying to sound alluring, and failing. Domingo winked at her. I knew he was thinking of the hottie he'd been with the night before.

'We'll leave with you,' Marge said. 'I'll just go and get Jazz.'

***

'So, what's the deal, soldier, what packing do *you* have to do?' Ana was cuddled up against me and I had my arms around her.

'I have just enough on me for a nice Goan meal, and I'd like to take my lady out for dinner.'

She smiled and held my face in her hands.

'Please don't invite the hairdressers,' I said, and she burst out laughing.

'I was about to tell *you* the very same thing.'

Ana was the one who spotted Marge gesticulating at us. She pulled at my sleeve and I pushed and shoved until I'd cleared a path for us.

I scanned the faces at the table where we'd been seated. There were more ladies in the group, but all of them appeared to be much younger.

'Can you spot her?' Marge cried out frantically. 'She doesn't seem to be here.'

CHAPTER 38

'Did you see Jazz, the lady who was with us earlier?' I asked Domingo.

'The sexy one, with the big boobs?' he replied, getting straight to the point, as usual.

I nodded.

'She was sitting in that corner, with Colaco and his gang. She's not there now?' he asked, looking in the direction of the table.

'No,' I replied.

'I told you to stay away from them, bro. They're into a lot of bad shtuff.'

'I know... I should've listened; but right now, I really need to find her.'

I turned to Marge.

'Are you sure she's not here?'

'I looked all over, Vic, can't spot her anywhere. I checked the loos as well, but she's not there either. None of them are.'

'Domingo,' I said, turning to him once again, 'take a look around, buddy. Can you see anyone who was with them earlier?'

He scanned the room for a while. The bar was on a slightly higher level and he had a decent vantage point.

'You see that guy near the entrance. I've seen him hanging out with them quite often.'

I clambered up onto a barstool. The lad in question had come up to our table and slapped palms with a few of them, including Colaco. Had his own girl with him now, which was probably why he had not hung around.

'Now this is what I want you to do,' I said, turning to the ladies. 'I want you to head back to Ronil and check if she's in her room. I'll take a look around here.'

'No, Vic, I'll stay with you,' Marge said.

'Marge, listen to me, I'll find her if she's still here. Now go back to the resort with Ana and check if she's there. If she's not, wait in your room until I return.'

'C'mon, sweetie, Vic will find her if she's here,' Ana said, and I could have kissed her. The last thing I needed at that point was a discussion about tactics. I knew what I had to do, and didn't want them around to see it.

As soon as they had left, I shoved my way over to the entrance.

The guy saw me approaching and I watched him cringe. His girl was with him, a pretty young thing who seemed to be really into him, and I knew he wouldn't want a scene in front of her.

'Buddy, I need to talk to you,' I said, placing my palms on the table. 'Can we step outside for a bit?'

'Later, dude, I'm kind of busy here,' he said. It didn't come out as cocky as he had wished.

'It's important, friend, and I'm asking nicely. I don't have to, y'know.'

He got the message.

'Be back soon, babes. I'll just find out what this guy wants.' She looked at me and I gave her a smile, a sweet one, I thought, but she didn't smile back.

We stepped outside and I walked him over to an area that was pretty isolated.

'Where is he?' I asked in a mild tone.

'Who?'

'Your buddy, David Colaco... where is he?'

'How the fuck should I know, men?' he replied.

I clipped him one on the nose. It wasn't a hard whack, but then this wasn't a hard lad by any stretch of the imagination. It must've stung, though, and his snout began to bleed.

'I'm going to ask you *one* more time, motherfucker, and then things are going to get nasty. Where is David Colaco?'

'How should I know, men?' he repeated, but his tone was whiny now.

I grabbed hold of his gut and began twisting the layer of flab that I found there. Pretty soon he was on the ground, squealing.

'Let me go, I'll tell you. I'll tell *yoooooo*,' he screamed.

I didn't let go, but I released my grip a bit.

'I saw them leaving around ten minutes ago. Colaco and Jimmy, his bodyguard, and that black guy who was with them.'

I twisted a little harder.

'And the woman? Was she with them?'

'Who?' he groaned.

'The woman... the *gori* who was sitting next to him when you came up to our table.'

'Yeah, men, she was, she *was*... now please let me go.'

'Where are they now?' I asked.

'I don't know, men, I swear on Jesus. I saw them heading towards the beach. That chick was so sloshed she could barely stand. Jimmy and Steve were almost carrying her.

'Thanks, buddy, I really appreciate the help,' I said, finally letting go.

'Fuck you, you bastard,' I heard, as I moved towards the beach.

***

I knew in my gut that something was terribly wrong. I'd sensed it during our first interaction in Parry's. There was something about him that was not kosher. He was, at the very least, a sociopath, with a deep-rooted belief that his wealth would allow him to buy his way out of anything. It had been a huge mistake on my part to invite him to join us. Jazz, I knew, was in serious trouble.

The blue SUV was parked outside the bar, which meant that they were still around. I sprinted up and down the stretch of beach near Parry's, but couldn't spot them anywhere, and so I retraced my steps towards the tall grass that lined the beach. It was an isolated spot and the thick vegetation provided ample cover. I should've checked there first, but hadn't thought of it.

The sky was overcast and I could barely make out what lay ahead. Luckily for me, I heard her groan, else I would have blindly walked into them.

CHAPTER 39

It was Baby Steve who spotted me first.

He was holding Jazz down by the chest and shoulders with one massive forearm and his free hand was clamped over her mouth to prevent her from screaming. Jimmy and another guy held her legs apart, while David Colaco, on his hands and knees, was preparing to take the plunge.

The black guy leapt to his feet as soon as he saw me, but by then it was too late for our Davy. He had a spongy arse, like a baby, I thought, as I dug the boot in. I felt his nuts getting squashed and knew they'd be in cold storage for a very long time.

Baby Steve was wearing a shirt and boxers and he didn't come at me as I'd expected. He moved off to one side, where his jeans lay discarded, and began rummaging in the pockets.

I moved towards him quickly. If he had a gun, I needed to disarm him before he could get a shot off. I felt a searing pain in my stomach and leapt back instinctively. He had a blade in his hand and from the way he held it I saw that he knew how to use it.

There are different ways to hold a knife, but many skilled fighters prefer a reverse grip with the blade pointing downwards. The grip is stronger, and you have the option of either stabbing or slashing. You can also conceal it behind your wrist, as Steve was now doing.

In the army we'd been trained to counter knife attacks, and the one thing I knew was that, good as you were, you were likely to get cut. The trick was to protect the critical areas.

In the current scenario, I also needed to factor in the other blokes in the fray. Colaco had curled into a ball and was lying on his side, whimpering. The other lad was kneeling over him and looking at me in a fearful manner. I didn't expect too much trouble from that quarter.

The pit bull was attempting to sneak up on me from behind; a mistake really, as he should've scooted off when he had the chance. I allowed him to grab hold of me, and the guy was as strong as I'd expected. He held me around the waist in a vice-like grip and lifted me off my feet.

The only problem, though, was that this wasn't the Bolshoi Ballet.

My right arm was free, though my left was trapped against my body. I was out of shape, what with the drinking and all, but the hate more than made up for this. I swung my elbow in a one-eighty-degree arc and caught him on the side of the head. His grip around my waist slackened, but he didn't let go. This was a sucker for punishment.

The looser grip gave me a little more space to manoeuvre. I crouched slightly, slammed my skull back against his face and felt his nose shatter. Then I swung my elbow once again with everything I had and this time it was lights out.

The thin little fucker had melted into the darkness, and there was only one more piggy to go.

He had slipped into his jeans (perhaps getting ready to scoot) and was still clutching his blade, but now he was trying to negotiate with me.

'Listen, brother, no hard feelings. You can take your friend and go.'

I grinned at him and moved in closer. You try to rape a semi-conscious woman, get busted in the act and then come up with a line like that? No hard feelings, brother, you can take your friend and go. Like that was ever going to happen. Hard feelings were all I had.

'Give me the knife, motherfucker,' I told him. 'Hand over that knife before I hurt you so bad, you'll be crippled for life.'

As expected, he didn't comply. I guess he figured that *he* was the one calling the shots.

I moved towards his left side, keeping one eye on the other two, who were stretched out on the grass. They didn't appear to be moving.

We had begun circling each other now. He'd realised that he couldn't talk his way out of this one, and he had a feral grin on his face, perhaps even relishing the contest. I know I was.

I made a feint with my left hand towards his groin and the blade scythed through the night air. It was a knife fight and I was expecting to be cut, but still the pain was intense.

By then, though, I had caught him on the left ankle with my army surplus boot. It was a crippling blow, the hardest I could manage in the circumstances, and I felt his bone shattering. He yelped like a mutt and the knife slipped from his hand onto the grass. He was on his arse now, clutching his ankle and staring at me in terror.

I kicked the knife away just to be sure. I had trained with blades, but I wasn't really a knife man. Besides, I knew he wouldn't be walking normally for a while.

He stared at me in silence, and this was probably why I let him go. I would've kicked his face in if he'd uttered a single word.

'Your shirt,' I said.

He did not appear to comprehend, and so I pointed to the cut on my forearm.

'Give me your shirt,' I repeated, and most of the buttons on that smelly vestment sprung free, owing to the speed with which he took it off.

'I'm sorry, man,' he said, as he handed it over.

I nodded. The rage had receded, but only as far as he was concerned. I ripped the shirt in two using my teeth and wrapped it around my forearm. The bleeding had not stopped and when I looked at it, I felt a bit queasy.

Jazz was sitting up, and I was moving towards her when I heard Colaco speak.

'You're going to pay for this, motherfucker. Just wait until my father finds out.'

I glanced at him and saw that he was crying. Snot oozed from his nose and he looked ridiculous. What I didn't see, though, was even a trace of remorse. Something primeval rose up inside me. It was fierce and uncontrollable, and I would've killed him if Jazz had not begun screaming.

'*Noooo*, Victor, *noooo*.'

It was only then I realised what I was doing. The prick had curled into a foetal posture and I'd been hammering away at his back and kidneys with my boots.

My head was throbbing and I waited for the bloodlust to subside. Jazz was moaning softly. I walked over and knelt on the grass beside her.

'Are you okay?' I asked. 'We need to go now.'

She clung to me tightly and began shivering. They'd worked her over pretty good as far as I could see. Her lips were swollen, her nose was bleeding, and her clothes were in tatters.

I thought of a girl, in another time and place, and shuddered.

'Jazz, we need to go now,' I repeated.

She was not responding, and so I made my tone harsher.

'Jazz *get* up, we can't remain here any longer. We have to go back to your hotel.'

She was on her knees now, trying to cover herself, which was hard, considering the state her clothes were in.

'Wait here,' I said, and walked over to the black fella.

He was nursing his ankle and cringed when he saw me approaching.

'Don't hurt me, man. I said I was sorry,' he whined.

'Your pants,' I said.

'What?'

'Give me your pants, motherfucker.'

They were off in an instant and he handed them to me. His jeans smelt like dog shit, but I didn't have a choice. Besides, I wouldn't be the one wearing them.

'Could you send for a doctor? My ankle is totally fucked.'

'I'll be back in a while, buddy, and if you and your friends are still around, what you'll need is a priest, not a doctor.

***

I thought I'd have to carry her, but she pulled herself to her feet, slipped into the jeans and covered herself with the rest of her clothes. She appeared reasonably composed now, though nowhere near as hard *kaur* as she'd been earlier. I held her by the waist and she slung an arm around my shoulder, and in this manner, we made our way to Ronil.

The elderly night clerk on duty had a blank expression on his face when he saw us hobbling in. I guess he'd witnessed quite a bit on the job over the years.

'Are you okay, ma'am?' he asked, and Jazz nodded. I was the one leaking blood on his floor, but he ignored me completely.

'Which room is her sister in?' I enquired.

'307, sir.'

The door was open and the TV was on mute when we walked in. Jazz went over to where Marge was seated, collapsed into her sister's arms and began sobbing.

'Where did you find her?' Marge asked.

'On the beach, with that rich prick and his friends. They were trying to rape her.'

Marge looked at me incredulously and then at her sister, who nodded.

'What happened?' asked Ana.

'I don't think they'll be doing any raping for a while, if ever.' I smiled. My own tremors had subsided and I thought a bit of Bogey-talk was in order.

'There were four of them,' Jazz whimpered; 'one of them even had a knife, but Victor took care of them.'

That was when Marge noticed the blood droplets on the floor. She looked at her sister first and then at me, and saw the shirt wrapped around my arm, which by now had changed colour.

'You're bleeding,' she shrieked, scaring everyone in the room, including me.

'It's nothing, just a tiny cut,' I replied, always the hard man when I had an audience.

Marge undid the makeshift bandage I'd fashioned and it turned out I was right. It was only a flesh wound, though it felt a lot worse. She pushed me into the bathroom and instructed me to undress and get into the tub.

'I'd love to, darling, but not tonight. I have a headache,' I said, and she cackled. This was one helluva dame.

Marge had a well-stocked medical kit in her bag (standard fare, I suppose, for tourists visiting India), and she had me patched up in no time. She was gentle and efficient and I gave her a kiss on the cheek for her trouble.

When we came out of the bathroom, Ana was staring at me. I'd heard her speaking to Jazz and wondered about the version she'd been given. It seemed to be a good one, based on her expression, and I was thankful she hadn't witnessed what had happened.

'Should I order something from room service, Vic?' Marge asked.

'Thanks, sweetheart, but we really need to head back. I have a flight to catch in the morning.'

CHAPTER 40

They came for me at daybreak, just when I'd begun to believe that I would get away with it. I was prepared, though, and when I heard the knock on the door, I was already dressed and set to go.

Ana was asleep on the bed and snoring gently. I hadn't spoken to her about what had happened, and I'm sure she'd conjured up a version in which I'd gone in alone, taken out the bad guys and rescued the damsel in distress. Which, if you looked at it objectively, wasn't far from the truth. The only problem was, I didn't know how badly I'd hurt them.

I moved over to the bed and woke Ana. She sat up instantly, which was unlike her, and I could see that she was afraid. The knocking was getting more insistent.

'What happened, Vic? Who's at the door?' she asked.

'Listen, babes, about last night: something bad might've happened. There were four of them, and I had to use a lot of force to stop them.'

'Did you kill someone?' she asked, her eyes filling up.

'Naah, nothing that serious, don't worry.'

But it got me thinking. I'd really had a go at Colaco and now I was praying I hadn't injured him permanently. I had been in such a rage that I had almost no recollection of what I'd done to him. All I could remember was Jazz screaming, and the look of revulsion on her face. In any case, there wasn't much I could do about it now, except to go out and face the music, which is what I did.

I waited until Ana was dressed and then unbolted the door. There were three guys in uniform standing on the steps.

'Is your name Victor Gabriel?' one of them asked. From the trinkets on his shirt, I placed him as the man in charge. We have the same affectations in the army.

'Yes,' I replied. 'What's the matter?'

His hand snaked up towards my collar, but I was ready for it. I slammed the edge of my forearm against his and by the grimace on his face I knew he was hurt, and more than a bit humiliated. He was a stocky fella with a fine moustache, and probably had a reputation for toughness.

With his other paw he made a half-hearted grab at my shirt, but I held him by the wrist and squeezed until he lost interest.

'Please inform me what I am being charged with,' I said evenly. 'You cannot barge in on innocent citizens and assault them without reason.'

I could see that my demeanour had unnerved him. In that line of work, they aren't used to folks talking back to them.

'There's a complaint against you for attempted murder. You'll have to come with us for questioning.'

'A complaint by whom?'

'David Colaco, sir, and two of his friends.' I noted the "sir" and was not displeased.

'Do you have an arrest warrant?' I asked, knowing that he didn't. It was too early in the day for that, and this was unofficial business.

'Sir, my advice to you is to come with us to the station. If you don't co-operate both you and your friend will be in serious trouble.'

I pretended to give this some thought.

'Okay, but give me a few minutes,' I said, and slammed the door on his face.

I watched them conferring from behind the curtain. One of them was pointing to his arm. He had noticed the blood-encrusted bandage on my forearm.

I made them wait for ten minutes, just for good measure. Ana was getting frantic and was bombarding me with questions that I didn't want to answer.

'Listen, sweetheart, I'll be fine. Now, I want you to take the first flight to Bangalore. I'll call as soon as I get things sorted out.'

'No, Vic, I'm coming with you,' she insisted. She was sounding hysterical now, which scared me more than the clowns waiting outside. The last thing I wanted was for her to get involved.

'Listen to me, baby, they don't have a case. I slapped that punk around a bit, because he and his buddies were trying to rape Jazz. Now he's gone and complained to his daddy, who's putting the screws on. Don't worry about it. I'll explain what happened, and I'll be back here before you even know it.'

I thought I sounded convincing, but I could see that she didn't believe me. There wasn't much she could do about it, though, as I gave her a quick hug and opened the door.

'Come on, *saab*, let's go,' I said to the fat constable, who seemed pretty chuffed to be addressed in that manner.

We walked towards the entrance, where they had a jeep waiting with a beacon and all. It was definitely a step up for me. The last time I'd been hauled in, it was in an auto rickshaw.

As we passed the lobby, I saw that the Braganzas were already up. Jack was slouched on the recliner, staring at me catatonically. He would need another infusion just to register what was happening. The witch gave me a spiteful look and then shook her head in disbelief. I grinned at her and raised my hand, and she turned away in disgust.

***

The police station was located in Porvorim, around half an hour from where we were staying. They led me inside and it turned out to be like any other cop coop in this part of the world. The walls were musty, the furniture decrepit, and even at that hour slobs in uniform waddled around like ducks.

But, like every other cop station I'd been to, the air was imbued with menace and a sense of violence to come.

***

I was escorted to the cabin of the inspector who'd been allotted the task of bringing me in. He was smallish and slender, and seemed to be an amiable fella. Also, I think he was a bit confused by my demeanour. I wasn't displaying any of the fear and servility that cops are accustomed to, and in his world, this could mean only one thing — that I had connections.

What he didn't know was that I was pretty nervous, though I tried not to show it. Being hauled in on a serious charge in this country was like playing Russian roulette. This was, of course, before the era of social activism and a more strident media, which at least tried to ensure that these upholders of the law were not breaking it too often themselves.

In those days, the only things that could possibly save you were a reputed lawyer, access to a senior cop or a very senior politician, none of which I had. In my case, they were all ganged up on the other side of the fence.

They didn't know this, though, and my apparent lack of fear bothered them. Also, the wound on my forearm had opened up and blood was dripping onto their floor.

The inspector, whose name was Furtado, asked one of the constables to escort me outside, where they made me wait for over an hour on a wooden bench.

Finally, just as I'd begun to nod off, Furtado stepped outside his office. He was accompanied by three constables, all of whom appeared far more impressive than the lot that was sent to bring me in.

'You will have to come with me,' he said.

'Sir, I want to know what I am being charged with.'

'You will be told all that in due course. Now, I want you to follow me,' he said, trying to summon up an air of authority. He nodded to the constables, who moved in. The fun was about to begin.

'I want you to know that I am an officer in the Indian Army,' I said, twisting the facts slightly.

This unsettled him, as I knew it would. In India the army is probably the one institution that still commands respect, especially from members of other security forces.

'You're an army officer?' he stammered, his confidence shaken. They did jobs like this all the time for men in power, but when the music stopped, as it did occasionally, they would be the ones holding the parcel.

I fished out my ID card and handed it to him.

'I fought in Punjab, counter-insurgency operations. I was awarded a Sena Medal for bravery.'

There was a long pause.

'Sir, could you please wait in my office?' he said after a while.

'Sure,' I replied, 'but would you ask someone to fetch me coffee?'

After I was seated and the coffee brought in, he excused himself.

'I have to make some phone calls,' he said.

'Sure,' I replied graciously; 'please take your time.'

***

And then began a waiting game. After almost an hour, he came back into the room, highly flustered, by the looks of it.

'I'm sorry, but we have to move you to the lock-up immediately. Some of my superiors are on the way, and they will be very upset if they see you here.'

I nodded. Big Daddy would've been working the phone for hours, and a lapsed ID and an attitude just wouldn't cut it for too long. Anywhere else, they'd have had me strung up by now, but in Goa everything moves at a leisurely pace.

I followed him to an empty cell at the back of the cop station.

'Please strip down to your underwear,' he said.

'No,' I replied.

He waited around for a while and then left. I'd begun to take a liking to the little bugger, but not enough to drop my pants for him.

CHAPTER 41

I was in there for less than an hour when I heard a commotion and rose to my feet.

They lumbered towards the cell: huge, brain-dead monsters, employed by the force to extract info or mete out justice.

The man who accompanied them was also brawny, but in a neat, tailored way that had IPS stamped all over him. A tidy collection of medals was pinned to his chest, and I knew that he ranked pretty high up in the department.

He was smiling at me, and it was a peculiar smile. I recognised the malevolence from where I stood and it unnerved me, though I tried not to show it.

'I need to speak to my lawyer,' I said, and it sounded weak even to me.

'You need to speak to your lawyer, do you? And what is it that you would like to tell him?' He was grinning now, clearly a man who enjoyed his work.

'I want to know what I am being charged with,' I said.

'You know, it's really funny when you think about it... you wish to know so many things, and yet I'm the only one here who will be asking questions.'

He waited until this had sunk in.

'So, why did you attack those boys?' he asked in a mild manner.

I remained silent. I knew he was just a catspaw, sent by those above to exact vengeance, and anything I said would only worsen my situation.

'*Ahh*... the silent treatment... then I guess we'll have to change our method of questioning.'

He made a gesture that was almost imperceptible, but it caused one of his men to dart forward and unlock the door of my cell. He then stood back with a sneer on his face as the three brutes sauntered in.

I thought about fighting back, but then decided against it. They would simply add a charge of assaulting policemen to the ones they already planned to pin on me, and in our part of the world this could very well be a death sentence.

They dragged me out of the cell by my arms and hair, and I willed myself not to resist.

'I am an army officer,' I screamed out as loudly as I could. 'I was awarded a Sena Medal in Punjab, fighting for this country.'

'You are an *ex*-army officer, if I remember correctly. And what do you want us to do about your Sena Medal, jump up and down and applaud?'

It was a fair question. And the guy had done his homework, I'll give him that.

'You know, this is what we dislike about you tourists. You come to Goa, hit on the foreigners and then pick fights with the locals. But this time you chose the wrong boy. You don't even know how deep a hole you've fallen into.'

They were hustling me down a long, dark passage. I hadn't even realised that the cop station was so big. It'd seemed quite unimposing from the outside.

'You're well aware that they were trying to rape a friend of mine. All I did was step in and stop them.'

'Really?' he said.

'Her name is Jaswinder and she is staying at Ronil with her sister, Marge... Margaret. You can check with them.' I felt terrible about dragging them into the mess, but at the time I *was* kind of desperate.

'We've already had a word with her, and that's not the version she gave us. She said that she had gone with them willingly, and then out of the blue you attacked them without any provocation.'

'She was about to be raped, and you know it.'

'Enough of this bullshit,' he snarled, and I sensed his nervousness. 'Two of those boys are in hospital, one of them very seriously injured, and you think you can just talk your way out of it?'

By then we had arrived at a largish cell. They shoved me inside and I went sprawling against the far wall.

'Remove your clothes,' one of the constables said, and this time I complied.

'*All* your clothes,' he snarled, when I was down to my underwear.

Well, fuck it, I thought philosophically, the way I'd been going, it had to end up this way.

They started out by throwing punches and kicks at me while the senior cop watched. This, of course, was not the full repertoire, merely the curtain-raiser for what was to follow. I had my face to the wall and had curled into a foetal posture to present as small a target as possible.

They then dragged me over to a metal table and strapped me to it, spread-eagled on my stomach. At least the Gabriel gems were safely hidden, I remember thinking.

I watched with a sense of déjà vu as one of the constables unrolled a leather strap and immersed this in a bowl of oil. This came as a slight relief. The strap was dipped in oil to prevent the skin from breaking, which meant that at least for now they didn't plan on killing me.

The brute walked around the table and I lost sight of him. I braced myself and let the fury consume me. If I ever got out alive, this IPS pig was a dead man, and David Colaco and his rich, fucking father as well.

I gritted my teeth and waited for the pain, knowing that I could withstand it.

In the army I'd been through commando training, and I knew that nothing could be so bad.

***

The commando training course called Ghatak (O) is mandatory for infantry officers in the Indian Army, and it was as close to dying as I'd ever been.

The IMA had been tough, but it could not compare in intensity with this course. We'd been told that it was one of the most arduous training programmes ever designed, and I believed it. There'd been a US Army Ranger doing the course with me, and he'd ended up as beaten and fatigued as any of us. Inhuman was how I remember him describing it.

The course is conducted in Belgaum, three times a year, and all army officers are required to complete it once in their careers.

It is spread over six weeks, and is designed to break you both physically and mentally. The long treks with weighed-down *paplus*, the hand-to-hand combat sessions, the obstacle courses and the sleep deprivation take their toll on every trainee. Even the fittest amongst us were collapsing with exhaustion by the end of the second week. This was the point of the entire exercise, as it was after this that the mind came into play.

We realised that human will is capable of performing the most amazing feats long after the body has given up. We were taught to cling on, to fight and persevere even after the last ounce of energy had been drained away. I had lost nearly ten kilos during my stint there.

I had always had a high threshold for discomfort, but going through this exercise taught me how to control the pain, to channelize and use it to my advantage, as I did in that torture cell in Porvorim.

***

There was a crack running along the edge of the concrete floor and I focused on this all through the ordeal. They were taking turns at the strap, ten minutes to a man, and after a few hours of this they were exhausted. The pain was immense, but it was a pain I knew I could handle. I muttered obscenities and curses, even cried out occasionally, but not once did I plead with them to stop. They finally gave up when not one of them could go on any longer.

Pain had never bothered me overly. Not that I relished it, but I knew that it was necessary, especially in the armed forces. True strength is only forged on the anvil of pain.

They waited until they'd regained their breath and then they dragged me to my cell. I wanted to walk back on my own, but found that I couldn't.

***

They'd dumped my clothes in a corner of the cell and I slipped into these with difficulty. It was a good sign, I knew. It meant that they didn't plan on working me over any time soon.

I dozed all through the day and night and for most of the next day as well. On the evening of the second day, one of the bozos came to escort me to the officer's cabin. It was a short walk, and I staggered all the way there.

'What's your name?' I asked pleasantly, as he helped me along. There's something about shared discomfort that makes buddies out of the most disparate kinds of people. Of course, I would've knocked him to the ground and stamped on his nuts, given half a chance.

'Why?' he asked, clearly nervous, and I knew the reason for this. After the treatment I'd received, the least he would've expected was fear, and here I was showing none of it.

'I need to include it in my formal complaint,' I said, just to yank his chain a bit.

***

The IPS prick, whose name was Kolekar, was also nervous, though he tried his best not to show it. Thankfully, on this occasion he didn't waste any time on sarcasm.

'We want you to give us a statement that you attacked those boys under the influence of alcohol. If you do this, we will apply a lesser charge and you will be let off lightly, perhaps without even jail time, given your army background. Otherwise, you will be booked under Section 307, which is attempt to murder.'

'The only statement I will give is about police coercion and brutality. Those boys were trying to rape my friend, a British national, and if I hadn't stepped in when I did, they might even have killed her. And now you are trying to protect them because one of them is related to a Minister,' I said, and watched him squirm.

'Listen, you bastard, don't give me any of your lip. I've dealt with riff-raff like you all my life. My advice is to do exactly as I say, or the consequences will be terrible.'

'For whom?' I replied. 'I was an officer in the Indian Army, decorated for gallantry. And you are an errand boy for a local politician, who is trying to protect a rapist. I have friends in the media who would love this story.' I was glad I sounded a lot more confident than I felt.

He was silent for a while and I could see the wheels in his head turning.

'Don't give me any of that bullshit about your army career. I checked about you, and you're nothing but a deserter.'

The interview ended and the brute escorted me back to my cell. This time around I went in silence.

***

I lay there all through the night, mulling over past events.

I knew that I deserved this, and perhaps more, given what had transpired. Simply put, it was bound to happen. All my life I'd been going off half-cocked, and it was only a matter of time before someone got seriously injured, or killed. Not that I gave a hoot about Colaco, Baby Steve or any of that ilk. They had got what they deserved.

The one person I felt sorry for was Ana. This was a woman, a girl really, whose only mistake was to fall in love with me. She was beautiful, wealthy, intelligent and kind, and she could've had just about anybody. But I was the fool she had chosen, and now she would regret it for the rest of her life.

The only thing I prayed for was that she would come out of this unscathed, that she would not be made an accomplice in something that didn't concern her in any way.

This was all that I hoped for. Even the thought of a stint in prison didn't bother me overly.

I was reaching the end of my tether, in any case.

CHAPTER 42

Dawn had just broken on my third day in captivity when I heard the thud of boots on concrete and rose groggily to my feet. If they planned on giving me another going-over, there would be blood spilt, and not all of it my own. This I promised myself.

The same guy had been sent to fetch me, and I could see that he was even more perturbed than the last time around.

'You need to come with me,' he said, almost apologetically.

He saw me flinch and added quickly, 'No, no, it's not for that. Someone has come to see you.'

'I was only following orders, sir,' he said, by way of an apology. I nodded. It was the same in the army.

I walked out of the cell and he followed. Very courteously this time around, he guided me to another office, a much larger one, with the name of the SP hung on a brass plaque outside the door.

The IPS prick was seated behind the desk, visibly anxious, but he was not the one my eyes were drawn to.

Ana was in the room, looking pale and distraught, and she stifled a gasp when she saw me. Marge and Jazz were there as well, as was Domingo. But it was not at any of them that I was looking.

It had been a few years since I'd last seen him and he had aged considerably. Outwardly, he was still dapper, but his hair was completely grey now, and his face was lined and haggard.

He turned to look at me, and then he glanced at his daughter. His expression was wary, not as cocksure as it'd been before, but there was absolutely no doubt that he was still the man in charge.

Ana sprang up from her seat and threw her arms around me. Marge rose, too, and came around and hugged me. Jazz remained seated, staring down at the floor. I didn't blame her for anything. She was who she was, and it was not that I didn't know this when she was hitting on me.

'What have they done to you, Vic?' Ana sobbed into my chest. 'Did they hurt you badly?'

'No, sweetheart, they don't hit as hard as you do,' I joked, but it wasn't easy. I was in considerable pain, and then there was the rage that consumed me every time I looked at the uniformed prick seated on the other side of the table.

'I want you to release him *immediately*,' roared Ana's father, and I saw the SP cringing.

'Sir, I can't just do that. There is a procedure. This man has been accused of a very serious crime. A young boy is in hospital battling for his life because of him.'

'That young boy and his friends were in the process of raping this lady seated here. I think you should take her statement as well.'

'Sir, that's not what she told us earlier. She gave us a written statement that she had gone with those boys willingly, and that this man, without any cause, attacked them.'

'That statement was given under duress,' Marge screamed. 'They came to Jazz's room in the middle of the night and threatened her, saying that they would plant drugs in her room and arrest her unless she signed a statement saying that she had gone with those arseholes willingly, and that Victor had attacked them without any provocation.'

Jazz sat in silence, tracing a pattern on the floor with her big toe.

'We also have a signed confession from a local drug peddler called John Obidiki that he supplied drugs to both the lady here and the accused two days before this incident.'

I couldn't place the name at first and then the ball slid in. John Obidiki aka Johnny Young. Seemed like all the rats were coming out of their holes. What kind of shit had we got involved in?

'This boy is a close friend of my daughter's, and he is being framed. Now, do you know who I am, or do you want me to spell it out for you?' The old guy sounded pretty impressive, I'll give him that. Even I was hanging on to his every word.

'Sir, I am well aware, but this is a serious charge and we cannot release him just like that.'

'Would you like me to speak to the Chief Minister? Perhaps you would like *him* to instruct you personally.'

At the time, Goa was ruled by a JP-led coalition, and Ana's dad was a senior functionary in the party. Last I heard, he'd risen all the way up to National Treasurer.

I wasn't too thrilled with what was happening, especially at what Ana had done to get me released. As far as I knew, she hadn't spoken to her dad in years.

The SP looked like he was about to start bawling.

'Sir, it's not that. I really *want* to help,' he whined, 'but this boy's uncle, Oscar Colaco, is a very powerful politician in Goa. He's currently a minister in the government, and he's very upset at what has happened. I cannot go over his head. Would it be possible for *you* to speak to him?'

I could almost see wheels turning in the old man's head. Ana was staring at him, as was everyone else in the room, and there was no way he could refuse under the circumstances. I almost felt sorry for him.

'Okay,' he said finally. 'Ask him whether he can come and meet me here.'

The cop seemed visibly relieved. He rose from his seat and left the room. Ana's dad insisted that I sit next to him and enquired about how I was doing.

'Not too bad, sir. I've been through worse,' I replied, and he smiled enigmatically, one badass to another.

Five minutes later, the cop came back into the room.

'Sir, he wanted to know your name?'

'VM Sadananda. Inform him that I'm the Party Convenor for Karnataka, and a personal friend of your Chief Minister.'

It seemed a bit much to me, but perhaps necessary under the circumstances. Maybe this was how powerful folks interacted with one another, while lower down the order we compared the size of our peckers.

The cop stepped out of the room once again, and when he returned, he appeared delighted.

'Colaco Sir confirmed that he will be here shortly. He said that it would take him at least half an hour because of the traffic.'

Ana's dad nodded and we sat back and waited. Tea was served and I was allowed to remain in the cabin with them, though I would have much preferred being back in my cell. We had little to say to each other, and the silence was oppressive.

***

The guy who finally showed up turned out to be David's dad and not his politician uncle, as we'd been told.

He stormed into the room with three large men in undersized T-shirts, which seemed to be the standard attire for bodyguards in their family. The SP sprang to his feet and indicated that he should occupy his chair. They appeared to know each other well.

The fat fuck hunkered down on the cop's seat and gave me a vicious stare. I smiled back at him sweetly.

'You bastard, do you know what you've done to my son?' he snarled. 'The doctors tell me that he'll be in hospital for at least six months.'

'Your brute of a son was trying to force himself on my sister,' Marge screamed out. 'If Victor hadn't shown up, they would most probably have raped and killed her.'

'*Shut up*,' he yelped in a high-pitched voice. 'You fucking bitches come to our state, fool around

337

with our boys, and then claim that you've been raped. Bloody whores, all of you. Go back to your own fucking countries.'

Marge was about to say something, but before she could, I rose to my feet. The cop took a step towards me, but it wasn't necessary.

I looked deep into his eyes, and luckily for both of us he got the message, and quickly. One more peep out of him and he would bleed. I knew this, and so did he.

He was back to being a fat fuck, with way too much to lose.

'Mr Colaco,' Ana's dad put in, 'I'd like to speak to you in private. Can we step outside, please?'

The arsehole nodded, grateful for the intervention. He was not the man he'd been when he first walked in. Besides, he was a businessman, and I'm sure he'd done the maths. There were many things they could cover up, but Jazz and Marge were UK nationals, and that would raise a stink if it ever got out. Political careers had been smothered for less.

They walked out of the room, the two rich men, and I played a staring game with one of the goons. It was hard for me, though. My face was battered and my eyes began watering, and I had to look away first. He seemed quite ecstatic about winning.

They were outside for a long time, and then Ana's dad came back into the room and summoned

338

the SP, who jumped up from his seat and followed him out.

I spent my time studying Jazz covertly. Her hair was wiry and she seemed old and jaded without the many layers of face paint. What the fuck had I been drinking?

The cop came back into the room, accompanied by Ana's father. With newfound authority, he gestured to the goons to leave.

'He's waiting outside for you,' he informed them.

'What happened, daddy?' Ana asked, and he beamed down at her, the top dog in the room, as always.

'We've decided not to file charges,' the SP answered; 'your friend is free to go.'

***

We said our goodbyes to the sisters, who insisted that they'd take an auto-rickshaw back to their hotel. Domingo said that he would accompany them. He had tears in his eyes as he hugged Ana and me. The kid had not uttered a single word in the cop station, but at least he'd had the balls to show up.

Ana's dad had hired a limo, and he insisted on dropping us back to the resort. I was seated in front next to the chauffeur, and when I turned around to make conversation, I saw that he had his arm around his daughter.

'When are you coming back to Bangalore?' he asked her.

'In a few days,' Ana replied.

'Should I send a car to the airport?'

'Yeah, dad, that would be great. I'll call and let you know.'

Back at Captain Jack's, Ana hugged him for a long time, and I could see that he didn't want to let her go.

'Thank you, sir,' I said to him. His eyes had filled up and he nodded at me, before getting into the vehicle.

CHAPTER 43

Ana had a chat with the crone and managed to convince her to extend our stay. It wasn't easy, though. She kept glaring at me while Ana was speaking, and I was hard put not to make funny faces at her.

We went back to our cottage, where I dozed for a few hours, and it was quite late in the afternoon when I surfaced. There were welts and bruises all over my body and I felt drained and listless. Ana stepped out for a while and returned with sandwiches and a quart of vodka. I was really grateful for this, as even the thought of *feni*, with its fruity, metallic tang, was making me gag.

We drank the vodka with water, and as usual Ana had one drink, and I polished off the rest of the bottle.

'Can you stay for just one more day, Vic?' It was already Wednesday, and I'd been due back on Monday.

'Of course,' I replied without hesitation.

After all, it was, in all probability, the last day I'd spend with her.

***

We remained in the room all through the evening, speaking occasionally, but mostly ensconced in a comfortable silence. The pain rose up intermittently and subsided as I lay on my side with my arm around her. I could sense that she wanted to make love, but it would have been very uncomfortable.

Sleep would not come easily, but the turmoil had receded. There was none of the rage or shame that had been there earlier. My mind was quiet, or perhaps only numb, and I hoped that the feeling would last forever. Finally, at around two or three in the morning, I dropped off.

The next day, perhaps for the first time ever, Ana woke up before me. My eyes opened and I turned around to see her staring down at me. She sobbed as she burrowed her face into my chest.

I tried explaining that the pain was not too bad now. It just appeared hideous. My back, buttocks and thighs were mottled and black and blue in several places, but other than this it didn't hurt too much, at least nowhere near as much as the previous day.

She wanted to stay in bed, ministering to my wounds, but I would have none of it. It was our last day together and I wanted to make it a memorable one, for both of us.

We headed out at eleven, and when we passed the lobby, I exaggerated my limp, just to give the Braganzas something to talk about. I knew that Jack was dying to have a chat with me, but the crone was seated beside him and so he said nothing.

We hired a beaten-up scooter and headed north. We'd both had our fill of the touristy-festive feel of the Calangute-Baga stretch, and wanted to go some place where we could be alone.

It turned out to be a long ride. I wasn't used to a scooter, and was not very familiar with the roads in Goa. I was also riding carefully, what with Ana perched on the back seat, clinging on to me as if her life depended on it.

We ended up in Morjim, which is a nice, secluded beach, north of Baga. Well, it used to be anyway, until the Russians got wind of it. Now I've heard that even the street signs are in Cyrillic.

We stopped at one of those rustic resorts situated right on the beach and rented a thatched hut for the day. Aside from the owners, a middle-aged Goan couple, we were the only ones staying there.

***

It turned out to be a glorious day.

We made love for a long time, and then took a walk on the beach. I would've liked to go for a swim, but the sea was rough and the salt would play havoc with the bruises. Being tough is one thing, but it ought to end at the line of idiocy. Not that I'd practised this too often.

We had a late lunch with the couple who owned the place and it turned out that they'd spent the better part of their lives in Bombay. They had both held down corporate jobs, but after their children had settled abroad, they moved back to Goa. Had not regretted it for a single moment, or so they claimed.

We stayed there till well past six in the evening, until the sun had set. We then bade goodbye to our hosts and made the trip back to Baga.

We made love in our room one more time, and then I held her close until she fell asleep.

***

I rose early, as I wanted to take the first flight out, whereas Ana had decided to extend her stay by a few more days. She awoke just as I had finished packing, and sat up on the bed. She was naked and I held her close, my face in her hair, imbibing her scent.

After a while, I pushed her away gently. I thought she'd be crying, but she appeared calm, almost serene. I was the one who looked like I would burst into tears, or at least that's the way it felt inside.

'I guess this is it, then,' she said.

I didn't reply.

'It was good for me, Vic, I want you to know that. Whatever happens, I will always feel this way about you.'

I forced myself to smile.

'And we'll always have Parry's,' I said.

We'd seen the film together, and she knew the line. She smiled at me, and it was a haunting smile, one that I will always carry with me.

'We'll always have Parry's,' she repeated.

***

When I stepped out of the cottage, it was pouring.

ACKNOWLEDGEMENTS

I would like to express my deep gratitude to the following people who have helped me on this journey:

My sister, Manju, whose unstinting support, suggestions and nudges, both subtle and overt, pushed me over the finish line.

Amma, who has always been my sounding board, my rock and my refuge when things get overwhelming.

Appu, for the title of this book, the edit suggestions and, most of all, for being the best man I know.

Colonel Digvijay Katkar, for providing me with a glimpse of army life, and for organizing the visits to the NDA and Amritsar.

Lucichi, Sandhya and Rosemary for your suggestions and support.

And Candy, for all those mugs of tea and coffee.

Lightning Source UK Ltd.
Milton Keynes UK
UKHW041001170919
349935UK00001B/10/P

9 781784 655013